JUNIOR GREAT BOOKS

SERIES 3

FIRST SEMESTER

◆ ◆ ◆

AN INTERPRETIVE READING, WRITING,

AND DISCUSSION CURRICULUM

JUNIOR GREAT BOOKS

SERIES 3

FIRST SEMESTER

THE GREAT BOOKS FOUNDATION

A nonprofit educational corporation

Published and distributed by

THE GREAT BOOKS FOUNDATION
A nonprofit educational corporation

35 East Wacker Drive, Suite 2300

Chicago, IL 60601-2298

CONTENTS

The Cat ran ahead until he came to some peasants.

THE MASTER CAT

Charles Perrault

A miller died, leaving as sole riches to his three sons his mill, his donkey, and his cat. The estate was easily shared out; neither the lawyer nor the notary was called in. They would soon have gobbled up the meager inheritance. The eldest son had the mill, the second the donkey, and the youngest only the cat.

The last was inconsolable at having such a poor share.

"My brothers," he said, "can earn a decent living if they combine together. But when I have eaten my cat and made myself a muff from its skin, I shall just have to starve."

The Cat, who heard these words but pretended not to, said in calm, confident tones: "Do not worry, master. Just give me a sack and have a pair of boots made so that I can go in the brambles, and you will find that you are not so badly off after all."

Although the Cat's master did not put much faith in this suggestion, he had seen him perform such ingenious tricks to catch rats and mice, such as hanging upside down by his feet, or lying in the flour bin pretending to be dead, that he decided that it might be worth trying.

When the Cat had the things he had asked for, he buckled the boots on smartly, slung the sack over his shoulder and, holding the cords with his forepaws, went off to a warren where there were large numbers of rabbits.

He placed some bran and sow thistles in his sack and, stretching himself out on the ground as though he were dead, waited for some young rabbit, still unused to the wiles of this world, to hop into the sack to get what was in it.

He had hardly lain down when his trick worked. A silly young rabbit jumped into the sack, and the Master Cat quickly pulled the cords and caught and killed him without mercy.

Swelling with pride in this achievement, he went to the palace and asked to speak to the King. He was taken up to His Majesty's apartments and, as he came in, he made a low bow and said:

"Sire, here is a rabbit which My Lord the Marquis of Carabas" (that was the name which he had decided to give his master) "has instructed me to offer you on his behalf."

"Tell your master," said the King, "that We thank him and that he gives Us great pleasure."

Another day he went and hid in a cornfield, again with his open sack, and when two partridges flew in, he pulled the cords and caught them both.

He presented these to the King, as he had done with the rabbit. The King again accepted the gift with pleasure and gave him some drinking money.

The Cat went on in this way for two or three months, taking game to the King every so often "from his master's hunting grounds." One day he heard that the King was to go for a drive along the riverbank with his daughter, the loveliest princess in the world, so he said to his master:

"If you will follow my advice, your fortune is made. All you have to do is to bathe in the river at the spot which I will show you, and leave the rest to me."

The Marquis of Carabas did as his Cat told him, without knowing what would come of it. While he was bathing, the King came by and the Cat began to cry at the top of his voice:

"Help! Help! My Lord the Marquis of Carabas is drowning!"

The King looked out of the carriage window and, recognizing the Cat which had so often brought him game, he ordered his guards to go quickly to the help of My Lord the Marquis of Carabas.

As the poor Marquis was being pulled out of the river, the Cat went up to the carriage and told the King that, while his master was bathing, some thieves had made off with his clothes, although he had shouted "Stop thief!" at the top of his voice. The rascal had really hidden them under a big stone.

The King immediately ordered the officers of his wardrobe to go and fetch one of his finest suits for My Lord the Marquis of Carabas. The King was kindness itself to him and, since the

fine clothes which he had been given set off
his good looks—for he was handsome and well
built—the King's daughter took an immediate
liking to him; and, by the time he had thrown
her a few appreciative but most respectful
glances, she had fallen madly in love.

The King insisted that he should get into the
carriage and accompany them on the drive.
Delighted to see that his plan was beginning to
succeed, the Cat ran ahead until he came to
some peasants who were mowing a meadow.

"Dear good mowers," he said, "if you do not tell the King that the meadow you are mowing belongs to My Lord the Marquis of Carabas, I will have you all chopped up into mincemeat."

The King did not fail to ask them whose meadow they were mowing.

"It belongs to My Lord the Marquis of Carabas," they answered in chorus, for the Cat's threat had terrified them.

"You have a fine piece of land there," said the King to the Marquis of Carabas.

"As you see, Sire," answered the Marquis. "It gives a wonderful crop every year."

The Master Cat, still running ahead, came to some harvesters and said to them:

"Dear good harvesters, if you do not say that these cornfields belong to My Lord the Marquis of Carabas, I will have you all chopped up into mincemeat."

The King, coming up a moment later, asked who was the owner of all these cornfields which he saw.

"They belong to My Lord the Marquis of Carabas," cried the harvesters, and the King again congratulated the Marquis. The Cat, keeping ahead of the carriage, said the same thing to all the people whom he met, and the King was astonished at the vast estates of the Marquis of Carabas.

At last the Cat reached a fine castle whose master was an ogre. He was the richest ogre of them all, for all the land through which the King had passed belonged to him. The Cat, having first found out who this ogre was and what he could do, asked to speak to him, saying that

he could not pass so near to his castle without having the honor of calling in to pay his respects.

The ogre received him as civilly as an ogre can and told him to take a seat.

"I have heard," said the Cat, "that you have the power of changing yourself into all kinds of animals; for example, that you can turn into a lion, or an elephant."

"That is so," said the ogre gruffly, "and to show you, I will turn into a lion."

The Cat was so scared at seeing a lion before him that he sprang up onto the roof, not without some danger and difficulty, because his boots were not suitable for walking on the tiles.

After some time, the Cat saw that the ogre had gone back to his original shape, so he came down, admitting that he had had quite a fright.

"I have also heard," he went on, "that you have the power to take on the shape of the smallest animals, for instance to turn into a

rat or a mouse. I must admit that I think that is quite impossible."

"Impossible!" roared the ogre. "You shall see!"

And he immediately turned into a mouse, which began to scurry across the floor. As soon as the cat saw it, he sprang upon it and ate it.

Meanwhile the King came in sight of the ogre's fine castle and said that he would like to go in. The Cat, hearing the sound of the carriage on the drawbridge, ran out and said to the King:

"Welcome, Your Majesty, to the castle of the Marquis of Carabas."

"What, My Lord Marquis," said the King, "this castle is yours, too? Nothing could be finer than

this courtyard and these buildings round it. Let Us see inside, please."

The Marquis offered his hand to the young Princess and, following the King, they went up the steps to the great hall. There they found a magnificent feast which the ogre had prepared for some of his friends who had been invited for that same day, but had not dared to come in when they heard that the King was there.

The King was delighted with all the virtues of My Lord the Marquis of Carabas, while as for his daughter, she was in raptures about him. Seeing his vast possessions and having drunk a few draughts of wine, the King said:

"You have only to say the word, My Lord Marquis, and you can become Our son-in-law."

With a low bow the Marquis accepted the honor which the King proposed, and he was married to the Princess on that same day. The Cat became a great lord and from then on only hunted mice as a relaxation.

The Fisherman and His Wife

Brothers Grimm

There was once a fisherman and
his wife who lived together in a
hut by the seashore. The
fisherman went out every
day with his hook and line to catch fish,
and he angled and angled.

One day he was sitting with his rod, looking into
the clear water, when suddenly down went the
line to the bottom of the water. When he drew it up,
he found a great fish on the hook.

The fish said to him, "Fisherman, listen to me.
Let me go. I am not a real fish but an enchanted
prince. What good shall I be to you if you land me?

I shall not taste good. So put me back into the water again and let me swim away."

"Well," said the fisherman, "no need of so many words about the matter. As you can speak, I had much rather let you swim away." So he cast him back into the sea. Then the fisherman went home to his wife in the hut.

"Well, husband," said the wife, "have you caught anything today?"

"No," said the man. "That is, I did catch a huge fish, but as he said he was an enchanted prince, I let him go again."

"Did you not wish for something?" asked his wife.

"No," said the man. "What should I wish for?"

"Oh dear!" said the wife. "It is so dreadful always to live in this hut. You might as well have wished for a little cottage. I daresay he will give it to us. Go and be quick."

When he went back, the sea was green and yellow and not nearly so clear. So he stood and said:

> Oh, man of the sea, come listen to me,
> For Alice, my wife, the plague of my life,
> Has sent me to ask a boon of thee.

Then the fish came swimming up and said,
"Now then, what does she want?"

"Oh," said the man, "my wife says that I
should have asked you for something when I
caught you. She does not want to live any longer
in the hut and would rather have a cottage."

"Go home," said the fish. "She has it already."

So the man went home and found, instead of
the hut, a little cottage, and his wife was sitting
on a bench before the door. She took him by the
hand and said to him, "Come in and see if this is
not a great deal better." They went in, and there
was a little sitting room and a beautiful little
bedroom, a kitchen and a larder, with all sorts of

furniture, and iron and brassware of the very best. And at the back was a little yard with chickens and ducks, and a little garden full of green vegetables and fruit.

"Look," said the wife, "is not that nice?"

"Yes," said the man. "If this can only last, we shall be happy the rest of our days."

"We will see about that," said his wife.

All went well for a week or fortnight. Then the wife said, "Look here, husband, the cottage is really too small. I think the fish had better give us a larger house. I should like very much to live in a large stone castle. So go to your fish, and he will send us a castle."

"Oh, my dear wife!" said the man. "The cottage is good enough. What do we want a castle for?"

"Go along," said the wife. "He might just as well give it to us as not. Do as I say."

The man did not want to go, and he said to himself, "It is not the right thing to do."

Nevertheless he went. When he came to the seaside, the water was purple and dark blue and gray and dark, and not green and yellow as before. And he stood and said:

Oh, man of the sea, come listen to me,
For Alice, my wife, the plague of my life,
Has sent me to ask a boon of thee.

"Now then, what does she want?" asked the fish.

"Oh!" said the man, half-frightened. "She wants to live in a large stone castle."

"Go home. She is already standing before the door," said the fish.

Then the man went home, as he supposed. But when he arrived, there stood in the place of the cottage a great castle of stone, and his wife was standing on the steps about to go in. So she took him by the hand and said, "Let us enter."

With that he went in with her. In the castle was a great hall with a marble floor, and there were a great many servants, who led them through the large door. The passages were decked with tapestry and the rooms with golden chairs and tables. Crystal chandeliers were hanging from the ceiling, and all the rooms had carpets. The tables were spread with the most delicious foods for anyone who wanted them. At the back of the house was a stable

yard for horses and cattle and carriages of the
finest. Besides, there was a splendid large garden
with the most beautiful flowers and fine fruit
trees, and also a park, full half a mile long, with
deer, oxen, sheep, and everything the heart
could wish for.

"There," said the wife, "is not this beautiful?"

"Oh, yes," said the man. "If it will only last,
we can live in this fine castle and be very
well contented."

"We will see about that," said the wife.

The next morning the wife awakened at the
break of day, and she looked out of her window
and saw the beautiful country lying all around.

"Husband," she called, "look out of the window. Just think if we could be King over all this country. Go to your fish and tell him we should like to be King."

"Now, wife," said the man. "What should we be Kings for? I don't want to be King."

"Well," said the wife, "if you don't want to be King, I will be. You must go at once to the fish. I must be King."

So the man went, very much put out that his wife should want to be King. He did not at all want to go, and yet he went all the same.

When he came to the sea, the water was dark and gray and rushed far inland, and he stood there and said:

> Oh, man of the sea, come listen to me,
> For Alice, my wife, the plague of my life,
> Has sent me to ask a boon of thee.

"Now then, what does she want?" asked the fish.

"Oh, dear!" said the man. "She wants to be King."

"Go home. She is so already," said the fish.

So the man went back, and as he came to
the Palace, he saw it was very much larger and
had great towers and splendid gateways. The
herald stood before the door, and there were
a number of soldiers with kettledrums and
trumpets.

When he came inside, everything was of
marble and gold, and there were many curtains
with great gold tassels. Then he went through
the doors to the throne room, and there was
his wife, sitting upon a throne of gold and

diamonds, and she had a great golden crown on her head, and the scepter in her hand was of pure gold and jewels, and on each side stood six pages in a row, each one a head shorter than the other. So the man went up to her and said, "Well, wife, so now you are King."

"Yes," said she. "Now I am King."

Then he stood and looked at her, and when he had gazed at her for some time he said, "Well, wife, this is fine for you to be King. Now there is nothing more to ask for."

"Oh, husband!" said the wife, seeming quite restless, "I am tired of this already. Go to your fish and tell him that now I am King, I must be Emperor."

"Now, wife," said the man, "what do you want to be Emperor for?"

"Husband," said she, "go and tell the fish I want to be Emperor."

"Oh, dear!" said the man. "He could not do it. I cannot ask him such a thing. There is but one Emperor at a time. The fish can't possibly make anyone Emperor—indeed he can't."

"Now, look here," said the wife, "I am King, and you are only my husband, so will you go at once? Go along. For if he was able to make me King he is able to make me Emperor, and I will and must be Emperor. So go along."

So he was obliged to go. And as he went he felt very uncomfortable about it, and he thought to himself, "It is not at all the right thing to do. To want to be Emperor is going too far; the fish will soon get tired of this."

With this he came to the sea, and the water was quite black, and the foam flew, and the wind blew, and the man was terrified. But he stood and said:

> Oh, man of the sea, come listen to me,
> For Alice, my wife, the plague of my life,
> Has sent me to ask a boon of thee.

...

"What is it now?" asked the fish.

"Oh, dear!" said the man. "My wife wants to be Emperor."

"Go home," said the fish. "She is Emperor already."

So the man went home and found the castle adorned with polished marble and golden gates. The troops were being marshaled before the door, and they were blowing trumpets and beating drums. And when he entered he saw barons, earls, and dukes waiting about like servants, and the doors were of bright gold. He saw his wife sitting upon a throne of solid gold, and it was about two miles high. She had a great golden crown on, set in precious stones, and in one hand she had a scepter, and in the other a globe; and on both sides of her stood pages in two rows, all arranged according to size, from the enormous giant of two miles high, to the tiniest dwarf the size of my little finger, and before her stood earls and dukes in crowds.

So the man went up to her and said, "Well, wife, so now you are Emperor. I hope you are contented at last."

"We will see about that," said his wife.

With that they went to bed. But she was as far
as ever from being contented, and she could
not get to sleep for thinking of what she would
like to be next.

The next morning as she sat before the window watching the sun rise, she said, "Oh, I have it! What if I should make the sun and moon to rise? Husband," she called, "wake up and go to your fish and tell him I want power over the sun and moon."

"Oh, wife!" said the man. "The fish cannot do that. Do be contented, I beg of you."

But she became most impatient and said, "I can wait no longer. Go at once."

So off he went, as well as he could for fright. And a dreadful storm arose, so that he could hardly keep on his feet. The houses and trees were blown down, and the mountains trembled, and rocks fell in the sea. The sky was quite black; and it thundered and lightninged; and the waves, crowned with foam, ran mountains high. So he cried out:

> Oh, man of the sea, come listen to me,
> For Alice, my wife, the plague of my life,
> Has sent me to ask a boon of thee.

"Well, what now?" said the fish.

"Oh, dear!" said the man. "She wants to order about the sun and moon."

"Go home with you," said the fish, "and you will find her in the old hut."

And there they are sitting to this very day.

"There was once an old man, as old as I am."

THE LITTLE DAUGHTER OF THE SNOW

Russian folktale
as told by Arthur Ransome

There was once an old man, as old as I am, perhaps, and an old woman, his wife, and they lived together in a hut, in a village on the edge of the forest. There were many people in the village, quite a town it was—eight huts at least, thirty or forty souls, good company to be had for crossing the road. But the old man and the old woman were unhappy, in spite of living like that in the very middle of the world. And why do you think they were unhappy? They were unhappy because they had no little Vanya and no little Maroosia. Think of that. Some would say they were better off without them.

"Would you say that, grandfather?" asked Maroosia.

"You are a stupid little pigeon," said old Peter, and he went on.

Well, these two were very unhappy. All the other huts had babies in them—yes, and little ones playing about in the road outside, and having to be shouted at when anyone came driving by. But there were no babies in their hut, and the old woman never had to go to the door to see where her little one had strayed to, because she had no little one.

And these two, the old man and the old woman, used to stand whole hours, just peeping through their window to watch the children playing outside. They had dogs and a cat, and cocks and hens, but none of these made up for having no children.

These two would just stand and watch the
children of the other huts. The dogs would bark,
but they took no notice; and the cat would curl
up against them, but they never felt her; and
as for the cocks and hens, well, they were fed,
but that was all. The old people did not care
for them, and spent all their time in watching
the Vanyas and Maroosias who belonged to
the other huts.

In the winter the children in their little
sheepskin coats—

"Like ours?"
said Vanya and
Maroosia together.
"Like yours," said
old Peter, and he went on.

In their little sheepskin
coats, they played in the crisp snow.
They pelted each other with snowballs,
and shouted and laughed, and then they rolled
the snow together and made a snow woman—
a regular snow Baba Yaga, a snow witch,
such an old fright!

And the old man, watching from the window,
saw this, and he says to the old woman:

"Wife, let us go into the yard behind and make
a little snow girl; and perhaps she will come
alive, and be a little daughter to us."

"Husband," says the old woman, "there's no
knowing what may be. Let us go into the yard
and make a little snow girl."

So the two old people put on their big coats
and their fur hats, and went out into the yard,
where nobody could see them. And they
rolled up the snow, and began to make a little

snow girl. Very, very tenderly they rolled up
the snow to make her little arms and legs.
The good God helped the old people, and their
little snow girl was more beautiful than ever
you could imagine. She was lovelier than a
birch tree in spring.

Well, towards evening she was finished—a
little girl, all snow, with blind white eyes, and
a little mouth, with snow lips tightly closed.

"Oh, speak to us," says the old man.

"Won't you run about like the others, little
white pigeon?" says the old woman.

And she did, you know, she really did.

•••

Suddenly, in the twilight, they saw her eyes shining blue like the sky on a clear day. And her lips flushed and opened, and she smiled. And there were her little white teeth. And look, she had black hair, and it stirred in the wind.

She began dancing in the snow, like a little white spirit, tossing her long hair, and laughing softly to herself.

Wildly she danced, like snowflakes whirled in the wind. Her eyes shone, and her hair flew round her, and she sang, while the old people watched and wondered, and thanked God.

This is what she sang:

"No warm blood in me doth glow,
  Water in my veins doth flow;
  Yet I'll laugh and sing and play
  By frosty night and frosty day—
  Little daughter of the Snow.

"But whenever I do know
  That you love me little, then
  I shall melt away again.
  Back into the sky I'll go—
  Little daughter of the Snow."

"God of mine, isn't she beautiful!" said the old man. "Run, wife, and fetch a blanket to wrap her in while you make clothes for her."

The old woman fetched a blanket, and put it round the shoulders of the little snow girl. And the old man picked her up, and she put her little cold arms round his neck.

"You must not keep me too warm," she said.

Well, they took her into the hut, and she lay on a bench in the corner farthest from the stove, while the old woman made her a little coat.

The old man went out to buy a fur hat and boots from a neighbor for the little girl. The neighbor laughed at the old man; but a rouble

is a rouble everywhere, and no one turns it
from the door, and so he sold the old man a little
fur hat, and a pair of little red boots with fur
round the tops.

Then they dressed the little snow girl.

"Too hot, too hot," said the little snow girl.
"I must go out into the cool night."

"But you must go to sleep now," said the
old woman.

"By frosty night and frosty day," sang the little girl. "No, I will play by myself in the yard all night, and in the morning I'll play in the road with the children."

Nothing the old people said could change her mind.

"I am the little daughter of the Snow," she replied to everything, and she ran out into the yard into the snow.

How she danced and ran about in the moonlight on the white frozen snow!

The old people watched her and watched her. At last they went to bed, but more than once the old man got up in the night to make sure she was still there. And there she was, running about in the yard, chasing her shadow in the moonlight and throwing snowballs at the stars.

In the morning she came in, laughing, to have breakfast with the old people. She showed them how to make porridge for her, and that was very simple. They had only to take a piece of ice and crush it up in a little wooden bowl.

Then after breakfast she ran out in the road, to join the other children. And the old people watched her. Oh, proud they were, I can tell

you, to see a little
girl of their own out there
playing in the road! They fairly longed for a
sledge to come driving by, so that they could run
out into the road and call to the little snow girl
to be careful.

And the little snow girl played in the snow
with the other children. How she played!
She could run faster than any of them. Her
little red boots flashed as she ran about. Not
one of the other children was a match for
her at snowballing. And when the children
began making a snow woman, a Baba Yaga,

you would have thought the little daughter of the Snow would have died of laughing. She laughed and laughed, like ringing peals on little glass bells. But she helped in the making of the snow woman, only laughing all the time.

When it was done, all the children threw snowballs at it, till it fell to pieces. And the little snow girl laughed and laughed, and was so quick she threw more snowballs than any of them.

The old man and the old woman watched her, and were very proud.

"She is all our own," said the old woman.

"Our little white pigeon," said the old man.

In the evening she had another bowl of ice-porridge, and then she went off again to play by herself in the yard.

"You'll be tired, my dear," says the old man.

"You'll sleep in the hut tonight, won't you, my love," says the old woman, "after running about all day long?"

But the little daughter of the Snow only laughed. "By frosty night and frosty day," she sang, and ran out of the door, laughing back at them with shining eyes.

And so it went on all through the winter. The little daughter of the Snow was singing and laughing and dancing all the time. She always ran out into the night and played by herself till dawn. Then she'd come in and

have her ice-porridge. Then she'd play with
the children. Then she'd have ice-porridge again,
and off she would go, out into the night.

She was very good. She did everything the old
woman told her. Only she would never sleep
indoors. All the children of the village loved her.
They did not know how they had ever played
without her.

It went on so till just about this time of year.
Perhaps it was a little earlier. Anyhow the snow
was melting, and you could get about the paths.
Often the children went together a little way
into the forest in the sunny part of the day. The
little snow girl went with them. It would have
been no fun without her.

And then one day they went too far into the
wood, and when they said they were going to
turn back, the little snow girl tossed her head
under her little fur hat, and ran on laughing
among the trees. The other children were afraid
to follow her. It was getting dark. They waited
as long as they dared, and then they ran home,
holding each other's hands.

And there was the little daughter of the Snow
out in the forest alone.

She looked back for the others, and could
not see them. She climbed up into a tree, but
the other trees were thick round her, and
she could not see farther than when she was
on the ground.

She called out from the tree:

"Ai, ai, little friends, have pity on the little
snow girl."

⋯

An old brown bear heard her, and came shambling up on his heavy paws.

"What are you crying about, little daughter of the Snow?"

"O big bear," says the little snow girl, "how can I help crying? I have lost my way, and dusk is falling, and all my little friends are gone."

"I will take you home," says the old brown bear.

"O big bear," says the little snow girl. "I am afraid of you. I think you would eat me. I would rather go home with someone else."

So the bear shambled away and left her.

An old gray wolf heard her, and came galloping up on his swift feet. He stood under the tree and asked:

"What are you crying about, little daughter of the Snow?"

"O gray wolf," says the little snow girl, "how can I help crying? I have lost my way, and it is getting dark, and all my little friends are gone."

"I will take you home," says the old gray wolf.

"O gray wolf," says the little snow girl, "I am afraid of you. I think you would eat me. I would rather go home with someone else."

•••

So the wolf galloped away and left her.

An old red fox heard her, and came running
up to the tree on his little pads. He called
out cheerfully:

"What are you crying about, little daughter of
the Snow?"

"O red fox," says the little snow girl, "how can
I help crying? I have lost my way, and it is quite
dark, and all my little friends are gone."

"I will take you home," says the old red fox.

"O red fox," says the little snow girl, "I am not
afraid of you. I do not think you will eat me. I
will go home with you, if you will take me."

So she scrambled down from the tree, and
she held the fox by the hair of his back, and they
ran together through the dark forest. Presently
they saw the lights in the windows of the huts,
and in a few minutes they were at the door
of the hut that belonged to the old man and the
old woman.

And there were the old man and the old
woman crying and lamenting.

"Oh, what has become of our little snow girl?"

"Oh, where is our little white pigeon?"

"Here I am,"
says the little snow girl.
"The kind red fox has brought me home.
You must shut up the dogs."

The old man shut up the dogs.

"We are very grateful to you," says he to
the fox.

"Are you really?" says the old red fox. "For I
am very hungry."

"Here is a nice crust for you," says the old
woman.

"Oh," says the fox, "but what I would like
would be a nice plump hen. After all, your little
snow girl is worth a nice plump hen."

"Very well," says the old woman, but she
grumbles to her husband.

"Husband," says she, "we have our little girl again."

"We have," says he. "Thanks be for that."

"It seems waste to give away a good plump hen."

"It does," says he.

"Well, I was thinking," says the old woman, and then she tells him what she meant to do. And he went off and got two sacks.

In one sack they put a fine plump hen, and in the other they put the fiercest of the dogs. They took the bags outside and called to the fox. The old red fox came up to them, licking his lips, because he was so hungry.

They opened one sack, and out the hen fluttered. The old red fox was just going to seize her, when they opened the other sack, and out jumped the fierce dog. The poor fox saw his eyes flashing in the dark, and was so frightened that he ran all the way back into the deep forest, and never had the hen at all.

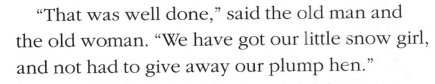

"That was well done," said the old man and
the old woman. "We have got our little snow girl,
and not had to give away our plump hen."

Then they heard the little snow girl singing
in the hut. This is what she sang:

"Old ones, old ones, now I know
Less you love me than a hen,
I shall go away again.
Goodbye, ancient ones, goodbye,
Back I go across the sky;
To my motherkin I go—
Little daughter of the Snow."

They ran into the house. There was a little pool of water in front of the stove, and a fur hat, and a little coat, and little red boots were lying in it. And yet it seemed to the old man and the old woman that they saw the little snow girl, with her bright eyes and her long hair, dancing in the room.

"Do not go! do not go!" they begged, and already they could hardly see the little dancing girl.

But they heard her laughing, and they heard her song:

"Old ones, old ones, now I know
  Less you love me than a hen,
  I shall melt away again.
  To my motherkin I go—
  Little daughter of the Snow."

And just then the door blew open from the yard, and a cold wind filled the room, and the little daughter of the Snow was gone.

"You always used to say something else, grandfather," said Maroosia.

Old Peter patted her head. "I haven't forgotten," he said, and went on.

The little snow girl leapt into the arms of
Frost her father and Snow her mother, and they
carried her away over the stars to the far north,
and there she plays all through the summer on
the frozen seas. In winter she comes back to
Russia, and some day, you know, when you are
making a snow woman, you may find the little
daughter of the Snow standing there instead.

"Wouldn't that be lovely!" said Maroosia.
Vanya thought for a minute, and then he said:
"I'd love her much more than a hen."

"Do you imagine this is the whole of the world?"

THE UGLY DUCKLING

Hans Christian Andersen

It was so lovely in the country—it was summer! The wheat was yellow, the oats were green, the hay was stacked in the green meadows, and down there the stork went tiptoeing on his red legs, jabbering Egyptian, a language his mother had taught him. Round about the fields and meadows were great forests, and in the midst of those forests lay deep lakes. Yes, it was indeed lovely in the country! Bathed in sunshine there stood an old manor house, surrounded by a deep moat, and from the walls down to the water's edge the bank was covered with great wild rhubarb leaves so high that little children

could stand upright under the biggest of them.
The place was as much of a wilderness as the
densest wood, and there sat a duck on her nest;
she was busy hatching her ducklings, but she
was almost tired of it, because sitting is such
a tedious business, and she had very few callers.
The other ducks thought it more fun to swim
about in the moat than to come and have a
gossip with her under a wild rhubarb leaf.

At last one eggshell after another began to
crack open. "Cheep, cheep!" All the yolks had
come to life and were sticking out their heads.

"Quack, quack," said the duck, and all her
ducklings came scurrying out as fast as they
could, looking about under the green
leaves, and their mother let
them look as much as they
liked, because green
is good for
the eyes.

"How big the world is!" said all the ducklings, for they felt much more comfortable now than when they were lying in the egg.

"Do you imagine this is the whole of the world?" asked their mother. "It goes far beyond the other side of the garden, right into the Rector's field, but I've never been there yet. I hope you're all here," she went on, and hoisted herself up. "No, I haven't got all of you even now; the biggest egg is still there. I wonder how much longer it will take! I'm getting rather bored with the whole thing." And she squatted down again on the nest.

"Well, how are you getting on?" asked an old duck who came to call on her.

"That last egg is taking an awfully long time," said the brooding duck. "It won't break; but let me show you the others, they're the sweetest ducklings I've ever seen. They are all exactly like their father; the scamp—he never comes to see me!"

"Let me look at the egg that won't break," said the old duck. "You may be sure it's a turkey's egg. I was fooled like that once, and the trouble and bother I had with those youngsters, because they were actually afraid of the water! I simply couldn't get them to go in! I quacked at them and I snapped at them, but it was no use. Let me see the egg—of course it's a turkey's egg. Leave it alone, and teach the other children to swim."

"Oh, well, if I've taken so much trouble I may just as well sit a little longer," said the duck.

"Please yourself," said the old duck, and she waddled off.

At last the big egg cracked. "Cheep, cheep!" said the youngster, scrambling out; he was so big and ugly! The duck looked at him: "What a frightfully big duckling that one is," she said. "None of the others looked like that! Could he possibly be a turkey chick? We'll soon find out; he'll have to go into the water, even if I have to kick him in myself!"

The next day the weather was simply glorious; the sun shone on all the wild rhubarb plants. Mother Duck appeared with her family down by the moat. Splash! There she was in the water! "Quack, quack," she said, and one duckling after another plumped in. The water closed over their heads, but they were up again in a second and floated beautifully. Their legs worked of

their own accord; they were all out in the water
now, and even the ugly gray creature was
swimming along with them.

"That's no turkey!" she said. "Look how nicely
he uses his legs, and how straight he holds
himself! He's my own flesh and blood, I tell you.

He isn't really so bad when you take a good look
at him. Quack, quack—come along with me, I'll
bring you out into the world and introduce you
to the duckyard, but keep close to me or you
may get stepped on, and look out for the cat!"

So they made their entrance into the duckyard.
What a pandemonium there was! Two families
were quarreling over an eel's head; but in the
end the cat got it.

"There you are, that's the way of the world!" said Mother Duck, licking her lips, for she did so want the eel's head herself. "Now use your legs," she said. "Move about briskly and curtsey with your necks to the old duck over there; she is the most aristocratic person here, and of Spanish blood, that's why she is so stout; and be sure to observe that red rag round her leg. It's a great distinction, and the highest honor that can be bestowed upon a duck; it means that her owner wishes to keep her, and that she is to be specially noticed by man and beast. Now hurry! Don't turn your toes in; a well-brought-up duckling turns his toes out just as father and mother do—like that. That's right! Now make a deep curtsey with your necks and say, 'Quack, quack!' "

And they did as they were told; but the other ducks all round about looked at them and said out loud, "There now! have we got to have that crowd too? As if there weren't enough of us already; and ugh! what a dreadful-looking creature that duckling is! We won't put up with him." And immediately a duck rushed at him and bit him in the neck.

"Leave him alone," said the mother. "He's not bothering any of you."

"I know," said the duck who had bitten him, "but he's too big and odd. What he wants is a good smacking."

"Those are pretty children you've got, Mother," said the old duck with the rag round her leg. "They are all nice-looking except that one—he didn't turn out so well. I wish he could be made all over again!"

"That can't be done, Your Grace," said Mother Duck. "He's not handsome, but he's as good as gold, and he swims as well as any of the others, I daresay even a little better. I expect his looks will improve, or perhaps in time his size won't be so noticeable. He was in the egg too long, that's why he isn't properly shaped." And she pecked his neck and brushed up the little man. "As it happens he's a drake," she added, "so it doesn't matter quite so much. I think he'll be a strong fellow, and I'm sure he'll make his mark in the world."

•••

"The other ducklings are lovely," said the old duck. "Make yourselves at home, and if you find an eel's head—you may bring it to me."

So at once they felt at home.

But the poor duckling who was the last to be hatched, and who looked so ugly, was bitten and buffeted about and made fun of both by the ducks and the hens. "He's too big!" they all said. And the turkey-cock, who was born with spurs and consequently thought he was an Emperor, blew himself up like a ship in full sail and made for him, gobbling and gabbling till his wattles were quite purple. The poor duckling did not know where to turn; he was so miserable because of his ugliness, and because he was the butt of the whole barnyard.

And so it went on all the first day, and after that matters grew worse and worse. The poor duckling was chased about by everyone; his own brothers and sisters were downright nasty to him and always said, "I hope the cat gets you, you skinny bag of bones!" And even his mother said, "I wish you were miles away!" And the ducks bit him and the hens pecked him, and the girl who fed them kicked him with her foot.

•••

So, half running and half flying, he got over the fence.

The little birds in the bushes rose up in alarm. "That's because I'm so ugly," thought the duckling, and closed his eyes, but he kept on running and finally came out into the great marsh where the wild ducks lived. There he lay the whole night long, tired and downhearted.

In the morning the wild ducks flew up and looked at their new companion. "What sort of a fellow are you?" they asked, and the duckling turned in all directions, bowing to everybody as nicely as he could.

"You're appallingly ugly!" said the wild ducks. "But why should we care so long as you don't marry into our family?" Poor thing! as if he had any thought of marrying! All he wanted to do was to lie among the reeds and drink a little marsh water.

So he lay there for two whole days, and then came two wild geese, or rather ganders, for they were two young men; they had not been out of the egg very long, and that was why they were so cocky.

"Listen, young fellow," they said. "You're so ugly that we quite like you. Will you join us and be a bird of passage? Close by, in another marsh, there are some lovely wild geese, all nice young girls, and they can all say 'Quack.' You're so ugly that you might appeal to them."

Two shots rang out—bang! bang!—both ganders fell dead among the reeds, and the water was reddened with their blood. Bang! bang! was heard again, and whole flocks of wild geese flew up from the reeds, and—bang! bang! bang! again and again. A great shoot was going on. The men were lying under cover all round the marsh, and some of them were even up in the trees whose branches stretched out above the reeds. Blue smoke drifted in among the dark trees and was carried far out over the water. Through the mud came the gun-dogs—splash! splash!—bending down the reeds and rushes on every side. The poor duckling was scared out

of his wits, and tried to hide his head under his
wing, when suddenly a fierce-looking dog
came close to him, with his tongue hanging far
out of his mouth and his wild eyes gleaming
horribly. He opened his jaws wide, showed his
sharp teeth, and—splash! splash!—off he
went without touching the duckling.

"Thank heaven!" he sighed. "I'm so ugly that
even the dog won't bother to bite me!"

And so he lay perfectly still, while the shots
rattled through the reeds as gun after gun
was fired.

It was towards evening when everything
quieted down, but the poor duckling dared not

stir yet. He waited several hours before he looked about him, and then hurried away from the marsh as fast as he could. He ran over field and meadow, hardly able to fight against the strong wind.

Late that night he reached a wretched little hut, so wretched, in fact, that it did not know which way to fall, and that is why it remained standing upright. The wind whistled so fiercely round the duckling that the poor thing simply had to sit down on his little tail to resist it.

The storm grew worse and worse. Then he noticed that the door had come off one of its hinges and hung so crooked that he could slip into the room through the opening, and that is what he did.

An old woman lived here with her tomcat and her hen. The cat, whom she called "Sonny," knew how to arch his back and purr; in fact he could even give out sparks, but for that you had to rub his fur the wrong way. The hen had little short legs and was called "Stumpy."

She was an excellent layer and the old woman loved her as her own child.

Next morning they at once noticed the strange duckling; the cat began to purr and the hen to cluck.

"What's the matter?" asked the old woman, looking about her; but her eyes were not very good, and so she mistook the duckling for a fat duck that had lost her way. "What a windfall!" she said. "Now I shall have duck's eggs—if it doesn't happen to be a drake. We must make sure of that." So the duckling was taken on trial for three weeks, but not a single egg came along.

Now the cat was master of the house, and the hen was mistress, and they always said, "We, and the world"; for they imagined themselves to be not only half the world, but by far the better half. The duckling thought that other people might be allowed to have an opinion too, but the hen could not see that at all.

"Can you lay eggs?" she asked.

"No."

"Well, then, you'd better keep your mouth shut!"

And the cat said, "Can you arch your back, purr, and give out sparks?"

"No."

"Well, then, you can't have any opinion worth offering when sensible people are speaking."

The duckling sat in a corner, feeling very gloomy and depressed. Then he suddenly thought of the fresh air and the bright sunshine, and such a longing came over him to swim in the water that he could not help telling the hen about it.

"What's the matter with you?" asked the hen. "You haven't got anything to do, that's why you get these silly ideas. Either lay eggs or purr and you'll soon be all right."

"But it's so delightful to swim in the water," said the duckling, "so delightful to get it over your head and dive down to the bottom!"

"Yes, it must be delightful!" said the hen. "You've gone crazy, I think. Ask the cat, the cleverest creature I know, if he likes swimming or diving. I say nothing of myself. Ask our mistress, the old woman, as well; no one in the world is wiser than she. Do you think she would like to swim or to get the water over her head?"

"You don't understand me," said the duckling.

"Well, if we don't understand you, then who would? You surely don't imagine you're wiser than the cat or the old woman?—not to mention myself, of course. Don't give yourself such airs, child, but be grateful to your Maker for all the kindness you have received. Didn't you get into a warm room, and haven't you fallen in with people who can teach you a thing or two? But you talk such nonsense, it's no fun at all to have you about. Believe me, I wish you well. I tell you unpleasant things, but that's the way to know one's real friends. Come on, hurry up, see that you lay eggs, and do learn how to purr or to give out sparks!"

"I think I had better go out into the wide world," said the duckling.

"Please yourself," said the hen.

So the duckling went away: he swam in the water and dived down into it, but he was still snubbed by every creature because of his ugliness.

Autumn set in. The leaves in the woods turned yellow and brown: the wind caught them and whirled them about; up in the air it looked very cold. The clouds hung low, heavy with hail and snowflakes, and on the fence perched the raven, trembling with the cold and croaking, "Caw! Caw!" The mere thought of it was enough to make anybody shiver. The poor duckling was certainly to be pitied!

One evening, when the sun was setting in all its splendor, a large flock of big handsome birds came out of the bushes. The duckling had never before seen anything quite so beautiful as these birds. They were dazzlingly white, with long supple necks—they were swans! They uttered a most uncanny cry and spread their splendid great wings to fly away from the cold regions, away to warmer countries, to open lakes. They rose so high, so very high in the air, that a strange feeling came over the ugly little duckling as he watched them. He turned round

and round in
the water like a wheel, craned his
neck to follow their flight, and uttered a cry
so loud and strange that it frightened him.

He could not forget those noble birds, those
happy birds, and when they were lost to sight
he dived down to the bottom of the water; then
when he came up again he was quite beside
himself. He did not know what the birds were
called, nor where they were flying to, and yet he
loved them more than he had ever loved
anything. He did not envy them in the least; it
would never have occurred to him to want such
beauty for himself. He would have been quite
content if only the ducks would have put up
with him—the poor ugly creature!

...

And the winter grew so cold, so bitterly cold.
The duckling was forced to swim about in
the water to keep it from freezing altogether, but
every night the opening became smaller and
smaller; at last it froze so hard that the ice made
cracking noises, and the duckling had to keep
on paddling to prevent the opening from closing
up. In the end he was exhausted and lay quite
still, caught in the ice.

Early next morning a farmer came by, and
when he saw him he went onto the ice, broke it
with his wooden shoe, and carried him
home to his wife. There the
duckling revived.

The children wanted to play with him, but he thought they meant to do him harm, so he fluttered, terrified, into the milk pail, splashing the milk all over the room. The woman screamed and threw up her hands in fright. Then he flew into the butter tub, and from that into the flour barrel and out again. What a sight he was! The woman shrieked and struck at him with the tongs. Laughing and shouting, the children fell over each other trying to catch him. Fortunately the door was open, so the duckling dashed out into the bushes and lay there in the newly fallen snow, as if in a daze.

It would be too sad, however, to tell all the trouble and misery he had to suffer during that cruel winter. . . . When the sun began to shine warmly he found himself once more in the marsh among the reeds. The larks were singing—it was spring, beautiful spring!

Then suddenly he spread his wings; the sound of their whirring made him realize how much stronger they had grown, and they carried him powerfully along. Before he knew it, he found himself in a great garden where the apple trees stood in bloom, and the lilac filled the air with its fragrance, bending down the long green branches over the meandering streams.

It was so lovely here, so full of the freshness of spring. And look! from out of the thicket in front of him came three beautiful white swans. They ruffled their feathers proudly and floated so lightly on the water. The duckling recognized the glorious creatures and felt a strange sadness come over him.

"I will fly near those royal birds, and they will peck me to death for daring to bring my ugly self near them. But that doesn't matter in the least! Better to be killed by them than to be bitten by the ducks, pecked by the hens, kicked by the girl in charge of the hen-run, and suffer untold agony in winter."

Then he flew into the water and swam towards the beautiful swans. They saw him and dashed at him with outspread rustling feathers. "Kill me," said the poor creature, and he bowed his head down upon the surface of the stream, expecting death. But what was this he saw mirrored in the clear water? He saw beneath him his own image, but it was no longer the image of an awkward dirty gray bird, ugly and repulsive— he himself was a swan!

It does not matter being born in a duckyard, if only one has lain in a swan's egg.

He felt quite glad to have been through so much trouble and adversity, for now he could fully appreciate not only his own good fortune, but also all the beauty that greeted him. The great swans swam round him and stroked him with their beaks.

Some little children came to the garden to throw bread and corn into the water, and the youngest exclaimed, "There's a new one!" And the other children chimed in, "Yes, there's a new one!" They clapped their hands, danced about, and ran to fetch their father and mother.

Bread and cake were thrown into the water, and everyone said, "The new one is the most beautiful of all! He's so young and handsome!" And the old swans bowed to him.

That made him feel quite embarrassed, and he put his head under his wing, not knowing what it was all about. An overwhelming happiness filled him, and yet he was not at all proud, for a good heart never becomes proud.

···

He remembered how once he had been despised and persecuted; and now he heard everyone saying that he was the most beautiful of all beautiful birds.

And the lilac bushes dipped their branches into the water before him; and the sun shone warm and mild. He rustled his feathers and held his graceful neck high, and from the depths of his heart he joyfully exclaimed, "I never dreamt that so much happiness was possible when I was the ugly duckling."

He heard a voice crying out from the shadows.

THE MONSTER
WHO GREW SMALL

Joan Grant

Far to the South, beyond the Third Cataract,
there was a small village where a certain boy
lived with his uncle. The uncle was known
as the Brave One because he was a hunter and
killed such a lot of large animals, and he was
very horrid to his nephew because he thought
the boy was a coward. He tried to frighten him
by telling stories of the terrible monsters that
he said lived in the forest, and the boy believed
what he was told, for was not his uncle called
the Brave One, the Mighty Hunter?

Whenever the boy had to go down to the river he thought that crocodiles would eat him, and when he went into the forest he thought that the shadows concealed snakes and that hairy spiders waited under the leaves to pounce on him. The place that always felt specially dangerous was on the path down to the village, and whenever he had to go along it he used to run.

One day, when he came to the most frightening part of this path, he heard a voice crying out from the shadows of the darkest trees. He put his fingers in his ears and ran even faster, but he could still hear the voice. His fear was very loud, but even so he could hear his heart, and it said to him:

"Perhaps the owner of that voice is much more frightened than you are. You know what it feels like to be frightened. Don't you think you ought to help?"

So he took his fingers out of his ears, and clenched his fists to make himself feel braver, and plunged into the deep shade, thrusting his

way between
thorn trees in the
direction of the cries.

He found a Hare caught by the leg in a tangle
of creepers, and the Hare said to him, "I was
so very frightened, but now you have come I am
not afraid anymore. You must be very brave to
come alone into the forest."

The boy released the Hare and quieted it
between his hands, saying, "I am not at all brave.
In my village they call me Miobi, the Frightened
One. I should never have dared to come here,
only I heard you calling."

The Hare said to him, "Why are you
frightened? What are you frightened of?"

"I am frightened of the crocodiles who live in the river, and of the snakes and the spiders that lie in wait for me whenever I go out. But most of all I am frightened of the Things which rustle in the palm thatch over my bed place—my uncle says they are only rats and lizards, but I know they are far worse than that."

"What you want," said the Hare, "is a house with walls three cubits thick, where you could shut yourself away from all the things you fear."

"I don't think that would do any good," said Miobi. "For if there were no windows I should be afraid of not being able to breathe, and if

there *were* windows I should always be
watching them, waiting for Things to creep in
to devour me."

The Hare seemed to have stopped being
frightened, and Miobi said to it, "Now that you
know that I am not at all brave, I don't suppose
I'll seem much of a protection. But if you feel I'd
be better than nothing I'll carry you home,
if you'll tell me where you live."

To Miobi's astonishment, the Hare replied,
"I live in the Moon, so you can't come home with
me, yet. But I should like to give you something
to show how grateful I am for your kindness.
What would you like to have best in the world?"

"I should like to have Courage . . . but I
suppose that's one of the things which can't
be given."

"I can't *give* it to you, but I can tell you where
to find it. The road which leads there you will
have to follow alone. But when your fears
are strongest, look up to the Moon and I will
tell you how to overcome them."

Then the Hare told Miobi about the road he
must follow, and the next morning, before his
uncle was awake, the boy set out on his journey.

His only weapon was a dagger that the Hare
had given him. It was long and keen, pale
as moonlight.

Soon the road came to a wide river. Then
Miobi was very frightened, for in it there floated
many crocodiles, who watched him with their
evil little eyes. But he remembered what the
Hare had told him, and after looking up to the
Moon, he shouted at them:

"If you want to be killed come and
attack me!"

Then he plunged into the river,
his dagger clutched in his hand,
and began to swim to
the far bank.

Much to the crocodiles' surprise, they found themselves afraid of him. To try to keep up their dignity, they said to each other, "He is too thin to be worth the trouble of eating!" And they shut their eyes and pretended not to notice him. So Miobi crossed the river safely and went on his way.

After a few more days he saw two snakes, each so large that it could have swallowed an ox without getting a pain. Both speaking at the same time, they said loudly, "If you come one step further we shall immediately eat you."

Miobi was very frightened, for snakes were one of the things he minded most. He was on the point of running away when he looked up to the Moon, and immediately he knew what the Hare wanted him to do.

"O Large and Intelligent Serpents," he said politely, "a boy so small as myself could do no more than give *one* of you a satisfactory meal. Half of me would not be worth the trouble of digesting. Hadn't you better decide between yourselves by whom I am to have the honor of being eaten?"

"Sensible, very. I will eat you myself," said the first serpent.

"No you won't, he's mine," said the second.

"Nonsense, you had that rich merchant. He was so busy looking after his gold that he never noticed you until you got him by the legs."

"Well, what about the woman who was admiring her face in a mirror? You said she was the tenderest meal you'd had for months."

"The merchant was *since* that," said the first serpent firmly.

"He wasn't."

"He was."

"Wasn't!"

"Was!!"

While the serpents were busy arguing which of them should eat Miobi, he had slipped past without their noticing and was already out of sight. So that morning neither of the serpents had even a small breakfast.

Miobi felt so cheerful that he began to whistle. For the first time, he found himself enjoying the shapes of trees and the colors of flowers instead of wondering what dangers they might be concealing.

Soon he came in sight of a village, and even in the distance he could hear a sound of lamentation. As he walked down the single street no one took any notice of him, for the people were too busy moaning and wailing. The cooking fires were unlit, and goats were bleating because no one had remembered to milk them. Babies were crying because they were hungry, and a small girl was yelling because she had fallen down and cut her knee and her mother wasn't even interested. Miobi went to the house of the Headman, whom he found sitting cross-legged, with ashes on his head, his eyes shut, and his fingers in his ears.

Miobi had to shout very loud to make him hear. Then the old man opened one ear and one eye and growled, "What do you want?"

"Nothing," said Miobi politely. "I wanted to ask what *you* wanted. Why is your village so unhappy?"

"You'd be unhappy," said the Headman crossly, "if you were going to be eaten by a Monster."

"Who is going to be eaten? You?"

"Me and everyone else, even the goats. Can't you hear them bleating?"

Miobi was too polite to suggest that the goats were only bleating because no one had milked them. So he asked the Headman, "There seem to be quite a lot of people in your village. Couldn't you kill the Monster if you all helped?"

"Impossible!" said the Headman. "Too big, too fierce, too terrible. We are *all* agreed on that."

90

"What does the Monster look like?" asked Miobi.

"They say it has the head of a crocodile and the body of a hippopotamus and a tail like a very fat snake, but it's sure to be even worse. Don't talk about it!" He put his hands over his face and rocked backwards and forwards, moaning to himself.

"If you will tell me where the Monster lives, I will try to kill it for you," said Miobi, much to his own surprise.

"Perhaps you are wise," said the Headman, "for then you will be eaten first and won't have so long to think about it. The Monster lives in the cave on the top of that mountain. The smoke you can see comes from his fiery breath, so you'll be cooked before you are eaten."

Miobi looked up to the Moon and he knew what the Hare wanted him to say, so he said it:

"I will go up to the mountain and challenge the Monster."

Climbing the mountain took him a long time, but when he was halfway up he could see the Monster quite clearly. Basking at the mouth of its cave, its fiery breath wooshing out of its nostrils, it looked about three times as big as the Royal Barge—which is very big, even for a monster.

Miobi said to himself, "I won't look at it again until I have climbed all the distance between me and the cave. Otherwise I might feel too much like running away to be able to go on climbing."

When next he looked at the Monster he expected it to be much larger than it had seemed from farther away. But instead it looked quite definitely smaller, only a little bigger than one Royal Barge instead of three. The Monster saw him. It snorted angrily, and the snort flared down the mountainside and scorched Miobi. He ran back rather a long way before he could make himself stop. Now the Monster seemed to have grown larger again. It was *quite* three times as large as the Royal Barge—perhaps four.

Miobi said to himself, "This is very curious indeed. The farther I run away from the Monster, the larger it seems, and the nearer I am to it, the smaller it seems. Perhaps if I was *very* close

•••

it might be a reasonable size for me to kill with my dagger."

So that he would not be blinded by the fiery breath, he shut his eyes. And so that he would not drop his dagger, he clasped it very tightly. And so that he would not have time to start being frightened, he ran as fast as he could up the mountain to the cave.

When he opened his eyes he couldn't see anything which needed killing. The cave seemed empty, and he began to think that he must have run in the wrong direction. Then he felt something hot touch his right foot. He looked down, and there was the Monster— and it was as small as a frog! He picked it up in his hand and scratched its back. It was no more than comfortably warm to hold, and it made a small, friendly sound, halfway between a purr and the simmer of a cooking pot.

•••

Miobi thought, "Poor little Monster! It will feel so lonely in this enormous cave." Then he thought, "It might make a nice pet, and its fiery breath would come in useful for lighting my cooking fire." So he carried it carefully down the mountain, and it curled up in his hand and went to sleep.

When the villagers saw Miobi, at first they thought they must be dreaming, for they had been so sure the Monster would kill him. Then they acclaimed him as a hero, saying, "Honor to the mighty hunter! He, the bravest of all! He, who has slain the Monster!"

Miobi felt very embarrassed, and as soon as he could make himself heard above the cheering, he said, "But I didn't kill it. I brought it home as a pet."

They thought that was only the modesty becoming to a hero, and before they would believe him he had to explain how the Monster had only seemed big so long as he was running away, and that the nearer he got to it the smaller it grew, until at last, when he was standing beside it, he could pick it up in his hand.

The people crowded round to see the Monster. It woke up, yawned a small puff of smoke, and began to purr. A little girl said to Miobi, "What is its name?"

"I don't know," said Miobi, "I never asked it."

It was the Monster himself who answered her question. He stopped purring, looked round to make sure everyone was listening, and then said:

"I have many names. Some call me Famine, and some Pestilence, but the most pitiable of humans give me their own names." It yawned again, and then added, "But most people call me What-Might-Happen."

THE LITTLE HUMPBACKED HORSE

Russian folktale
as told by Post Wheeler

Across the wide
sea-ocean, on the further
side of high mountains,
beyond thick forests, in a
village that faced the sky, there
once lived an old peasant who had three sons.
The eldest, Danilo, was the most knowing
lad in the place; the second, Gavrilo, was neither
clever nor dull; and the youngest, who was
named Ivan, was called a dullard, because while
his brothers, after they had sowed their wheat
and threshed it, drove to town and went
merrymaking, he cared to do nothing but lie in

the corner on the stove and sleep. So the whole neighborhood called him "Little Fool Ivan."

Now one morning when the peasant went to his stack, he found to his dismay that someone in the night had stolen some of the hay, so that evening he sent his eldest son to watch for the thief.

Danilo, accordingly, took his ax and his hayfork and went to the field. On this night there was a biting frost and heavy snow, and he said to himself, "Why should I freeze myself stiff to save a little worthless fodder?" So, finding a warm corner, he lay down, wrapped himself in his thick fur coat, and went to sleep.

In the morning he saw that some of the hay had been stolen. He rolled himself well in the snow, went home, and knocked at the door till his father let him in.

"Didst thou see the thief?" asked the peasant.

"I heard him prowling not far off," answered Danilo, "but I shouted and he dared not come nearer. However, I have had a terrible night, thou mayst be sure! It was bitter cold and I am frozen to the marrow!"

His father praised him, calling him a good son, and the next night sent his second son to watch.

So Gavrilo took his hatchet and his long knife and went to the field. Now on this night it was raining, and he said to himself, "They say my brother is cleverer than I, but I am at least knowing enough to take care of myself, and why should I stand all night wet to the skin for the sake of a little dried grass?" So, having found a sheltered spot, he lay down, covered himself with his warm cloak and went to sleep.

In the morning he saw that more of the hay had been stolen. He went to a brook, poured water over his clothing so that it was drenched,

went home, and knocked at the door till it
was opened.

"Didst thou see the thief?" asked his father.

"I did," Gavrilo answered, "and laid hold of his
coat and gave him such a beating that he will
remember it. But the rascal tore away and ran so
fast that I could not catch him. But I have had
a night for my pains, I can tell you! The rain
poured every minute and I am soaked to
the bones!"

His father praised him likewise, calling him
a brave fellow till he was as proud as a cock with
five hens, and the next evening said to the Little
Fool Ivan, "Now, my son, it is thy turn to watch,
but thou art such a simpleton thou canst not

99

even keep the sparrows from the peas. It will be small use for thee to go."

However, Little Fool Ivan climbed down from the stove, put a crust of bread under his coat, and went whistling off to the field. He did not lie down as his brothers had done, but went about the whole field, looking on every side, and when the moon rose he sat down under a bush, counted the stars in the sky, and ate his crust with a good appetite.

Suddenly, just at midnight, he heard the neigh of a horse, and looking out from the bush he saw a wonderful mare, as white as snow, with a golden mane curled in little rings.

"So," said Little Fool Ivan to himself, "thou art, then, the thief of our hay! Only come a little nearer and I will be on thy back as tight as a locust!" The mare came nearer and nearer and at last, choosing the right moment, Ivan leaped out, seized her tail, and jumped onto her back, wrong side before.

The white mare's eyes darted forth lightning. She curled her neck like a snake, reared on her hind legs, and shot off like an arrow. She raced over fields, she flew like a bird over ditches,

she galloped like the wind along mountains
and dashed through thick forests. But run as she
would, and rear and snort as she might, she
could not throw off Little Fool Ivan. He clung to
her tail and stuck to her back like a burr.

At last, just as day was beginning to dawn, the
mare stopped and, panting, spoke to him with a
human voice. "Well, Ivan," she said, "since thou
canst sit me, it seems thou must possess me.
Take me home and give me a place to rest for
three days. Only, each morning, just at sunrise,

let me out to roll in the dew. And when the three days are up, I will bear thee three such colts as were never heard of before. Two of them will be Tsar's horses, of brown and gray, and these thou mayst sell if thou choosest. But the third will be a little humpbacked stallion only three feet high, with ears a foot long, and him thou shalt neither sell for gold nor give as a gift to anyone whatsoever. So long as thou art in the white world he shall be thy faithful servant. In winter he will show thee how to be warm, and when thou dost hunger he will show thee where to find bread. In return for these three colts thou shalt release me and give me my freedom."

Little Fool Ivan agreed. He rode the white mare home, hid her in an empty shepherd's corral, whose entrance he covered with a horse-cloth, and went home and knocked at the door till his brothers let him in.

When they saw him, they began to question him. "Well, no doubt thou didst see the thief! Perhaps thou didst even catch him! Tell us."

"To be sure I did," he replied. "I jumped on the thief's back and laid hold of the villain's tail, and we ran a thousand versts or more. My neck

was nearly broken in the end and ye may believe
I am tired!" So saying he climbed onto the stove
without taking off even his bark sandals, and
went to sleep, while his brothers and his father
roared with laughter at the story, not a word
of which, of course, they believed.

Little Fool Ivan kept the white mare hidden
from all other eyes. For three mornings he
rose at daybreak and let her out to roll on the
dewy meadow and on the fourth morning, when
he went to the corral, he found beside her,
as she had promised, three colts. Two were most
beautiful to see; they were of brown and gray,
their eyes were like blue sapphires, their manes
and tails were golden and curled in little rings,

and their hoofs were of diamond, studded with pearls. But the third was a tiny horse like a toy, with two humps on his back and ears a foot long.

Ivan was overjoyed. He thanked the white mare and she, released, curled her neck like a snake, reared on her hind legs, and shot off like an arrow. Then he began to admire the three colts, especially the little humpbacked one which frisked like a dog about Ivan's knees, clapping his long ears together from playfulness and dancing up and down on his little hoofs. He kept them hidden, as he had the white mare, in the shepherd's corral, letting them out each morning at sunrise to roll in the dew and spending many hours petting them, talking to them, currying their coats till they shone like silver, and braiding their golden manes.

Time went on (but whether it was three weeks or three years that flew away matters little, since one need not run after them) till it befell, one day, that his eldest brother, Danilo, who had been to town for a holiday, returned late at night and, missing his way in the darkness, stumbled into the shepherd's corral. Hearing a sound,

he made a light and to his astonishment saw the
three young horses.

"So—ho!" he thought. "Now I understand
why Little Fool Ivan spends so much time in this
old corral!" He ran to the house and woke his
brother Gavrilo. "Come quickly," he said, "and see
what three horses our young idiot of a brother
has found for himself!" And Gavrilo followed
him as fast as he could, straight across a nettle
field barefoot, since he did not wait to put
on his boots.

When they came to the corral the two fine
horses were neighing and snorting. Their eyes

were burning like beautiful blue candles and their curling gold manes and tails and their hoofs of diamonds and pearls filled the two brothers with envy. Each looked at them so long that he was nearly made blind of one eye. Then Danilo said:

"They say it takes a fool to find a treasure. But where in the white world could Little Fool Ivan have got these marvelous steeds? As for thee and me, brother, we might search our heads off and we would find not even two roubles!"

"That is true," answered Gavrilo. "We should have the horses, and not Little Fool Ivan. Now I have an idea. Next week is the Fair at the capital. Many foreigners will come in ships to buy linen and it is said that even Tsar Saltan will be there. Let us come here by night and take the horses thither and sell them. They will fetch a great price and we will divide it equally between us two. Thou knowest what a good time we could have with the money, and while we are slapping our full purses and enjoying ourselves our dolt of an Ivan will not be able to guess where his horses have gone visiting. What sayest thou? Let us shake hands upon it."

So the brothers agreed, kissed each other, crossed themselves, and went home planning how to spend the money they should get for the horses.

When the next week came round, accordingly, they said a prayer before the holy images, asked their father's blessing, and departed to the Fair. When they had gone some distance, however, they returned to the village secretly after nightfall, took the two fine horses out of the corral, and again set out for the capital.

Next morning, when Ivan came to the corral, he found to his grief that the beautiful pair had vanished. There was left only the little humpbacked horse that was turning round and round before him, capering, clapping his long ears together, and dancing up and down from joy. Ivan began to weep salt tears. "O my horses, brown and gray!" he cried. "My good steeds with golden manes! Did I not caress you enough? What wretch—may he tumble through a bridge!—hath stolen you away?"

At this the humpbacked horse neighed and spoke in a human voice, "Don't worry, little master," he said. "It was thy brothers who took

them away and I can take thee to them. Sit on
my back and hold fast by my ears, and have a
care not to fall off!" So Little Fool Ivan sat on his
back, holding up his feet lest they drag on the
ground, and laid hold of his ears, and the pony
shook himself till his little mane quivered, reared
on his hind legs, snorted three times, and shot
away like an arrow, so fast that the dust curled
under his feet. And almost before Ivan had
time to take breath, he was versts away on the
highroad to the capital.

When his brothers saw Little Fool Ivan coming
after them like the wind on his toy horse, they
knew not what to do. "For shame, ye rascals!"

shouted he as he overtook them. "Ye may be more clever than I, but I have never stolen your steeds!"

"Our dear little brother!" said Danilo. "There is little use denying. We took thy two horses, but we did so with no thought of wrong to thee. As thou knowest, this has been a poor season with our crops and a bad harvest, and for despair I and Gavrilo have been like to hang ourselves. When we came by chance upon these two steeds, we considered that thou hadst little knowledge of bargaining and tracing, and doubtless knew not their worth, whereas we could get for them at least a thousand roubles at the Fair. With this money we could help our little father, as thou wouldst wish, and we purposed to buy besides for thee a red cap and new boots with red heels. So if we have erred, do thou forgive us."

"Well," answered Little Fool Ivan, "thy words sound fair enough. If this was your thought, go and sell my two horses, but I will go with you." So, though they wished him well strangled, the two brothers had no choice but to take him with them, and thus they came to the capital.

···

Now when they reached the marketplace where the traders were assembled, so wonderful were the two steeds that the people swarmed about them, buzzing like bees in a hive, till for the press no one could pass either in or out, and there was great commotion. Perceiving this the head man sent a crier who blew on a gold trumpet and shouted in a loud voice, "O merchants and buyers! Crowd not, but disperse one and all!" But they would not move from the horses. Then the head man rode out himself, in slippers and fur cap, with a body of soldiers who cleared the way with their whips, so that he came to the middle of the market and saw the horses with his own eyes.

"God's world is wonderful!" he cried, rubbing his head. "What marvels doth it hold!" And bidding the crier proclaim that no buyer should buy them, he rode to the Palace, came to the presence of the Tsar, and told him of them.

The Tsar could not sit still for curiosity. He ordered his state carriage and rode at once to the market, and when he saw the horses, tugging at their halters and gnawing their bits, with their eyes shining like sapphires, their curling golden

manes, and hoofs of diamonds and pearls, he
could not take his eyes from them. He examined
them on both sides, called to them with caressing
words, patted their backs, and stroked their
manes, and asked who owned them.

"O Tsar's Majesty," said Little Fool Ivan, "I am
their master."

"What wilt thou take for them?" asked the Tsar.

"Thrice five caps of full silver," answered Ivan,
"and five roubles beside."

"Good," said the Tsar, and ordered the money
given him. Then ten grooms, with gray hair and
golden uniforms, led the pair to the royal stables.

●●●

On the way, however, the horses knocked the
grooms down, bit to pieces their bridles, and ran
neighing back to Ivan.

Then the Tsar called him to his presence, and
said, "It seems that my wonderful steeds will
obey only thee. There is no help but that I make
thee my Chief Equerry and Master of my Stables."
And he ordered the crier at once to proclaim
the appointment. So Little Fool Ivan called his
brothers Danilo and Gavrilo, gave to them the
fifteen caps full of silver, and the five roubles
beside, kissed them, bade them not neglect their
father but to care for him in his old age, and
led the two horses to the royal stables, while a
great throng of people followed, watching the
little humpbacked horse who went dancing
after them up the street.

The telling of a tale is quick but time itself
passes slowly. Five weeks went by, while Ivan
wore red robes, ate sweet food, and slept his fill.
Each morning at sunrise he took the horses to
roll in the dew on the open field, and fed them
with honey and white wheat till their coats shone
like satin. But the more the Tsar praised him,
the more envious many in the Court were of him.

As the saying is, one need not be rich only so
he have curly hair and is clever; and because
Little Fool Ivan had succeeded so easily people
hated him, and the one who hated him most was
the officer who had been the Tsar's Master of
Horse before his coming. Each day this man
pondered how he might bring about Ivan's ruin,
and at night he would creep to the stables
and lie hid in the wheat bins, hoping to catch
his rival in some fault.

When this failed, he went to all those
Court officials who were envious of the new
favorite and bade them hang their heads and go
about with sorrowful faces, promising, when
the Tsar asked the cause, to tell him what
would ruin Little Fool Ivan. They did so, and
the Tsar, noticing their sad looks, asked:

"O Boyars, why are ye cast down and
crestfallen?"

Then he who had given this counsel stood
forth, and said, "O Tsar's Majesty! not for
ourselves do we grieve, but we fear thy new
Master of the Stables is a wizard and an evildoer
and familiar with Black Magic. For he doth boast
openly that he could fetch thee, if he chose,

in addition to thy two wonderful steeds, the fabled Pig with the Golden Bristles and the Silver Tusks, with her twenty sucklings, who live in the hidden valley of the Land of the South."

Hearing this, the Tsar was wroth. "Bring before me this wild boaster," he said, "and he shall make good his words without delay!" Thereupon they ran to the stables, where Little Fool Ivan lay asleep, and kicked him wide awake and brought him to the Tsar, who looked at him angrily, and said, "Hear my command. If in three days thou hast not brought hither, from the hidden valley of the Land of the South, the Pig with the Golden

Bristles and Silver Tusks, together with her
twenty sucklings, I will deliver thee to an
evil death!"

Little Fool Ivan went out to the stable
weeping bitterly. Hearing him coming, the little
humpbacked horse began to dance and to
clap its ears together for joy, but as soon as he
saw his master's tears he almost began to sob
himself. "Why art thou not merry, little master?"
he asked. "Why does thy head hang lower
than thy shoulders?"

Ivan embraced and kissed the little horse, and
told him the task the Tsar had laid upon him.
"Do not weep," said the pony; "I can help thee.
Nor is this service so hard a one. Go thou to
the Tsar and ask of him a bucket of golden corn,
a bucket of silver wheat, and a silken lasso."

So Ivan went before the Tsar and asked, as
he had been bidden, for the wheat, the corn, and
the silken lasso, and brought them back to the
stables. "Now," said the little humpbacked horse,
"lie down and sleep, for the morning holds
more wisdom than the evening."

Little Fool Ivan lay down to sleep, and next
morning the pony waked him at dawn. "Mount

me now," he said, "with thy grain and thy silken
rope, and we will be off, for the way is far."

Ivan put the silver wheat and the golden corn
into stout bags, slung them across the pony's
neck, and with his silken lasso wound about his
waist, mounted, and the little humpbacked horse
darted away like an eagle. He scoured wide
plains, leaped across swift rivers, and sped along
mountain ridges, and after running without pause
for a day and a night, he stopped in a deep
valley on the edge of a dreary wood, and said,
"Little master, this is the Land of the South,

and in this valley lives the Pig with the Golden
Bristles. She comes each day to root in this
forest. Take thou the golden corn and the silver
wheat and pour them on the ground in two piles,
at some distance apart, and conceal thyself.
When the Pig comes she will run to the corn,
but the sucklings will begin to eat the wheat,
and while the mother is not by, thou mayst
secure them. Bring them to me and tie them to
my saddle with the silken lasso and I will bear
thee back. As for the Pig, she will follow her
sucklings."

Little Fool Ivan did all as the little horse bade
him. He entered the forest, put the corn and
wheat into two piles, hid himself in a thicket near
the latter, and rested till evening, when there came
a sound of grunting and the Pig with the Golden
Bristles and Silver Tusks led her young into the
forest. She saw the corn, and at once began to eat
it, while the twenty sucklings ran to the wheat.
He caught them, one by one, tied them with
the silken lasso, and, hastening to the little horse,
made them fast to his saddlebow. Scarce had
he mounted when the Pig perceived them, and
seeing her sucklings borne away, came running

after them, erecting her golden bristles and
gnashing her silver tusks.

The little humpbacked horse sped away like a
flash back along the road they had come, with
the Pig pursuing them, and, after running without
stop for a night and a day, they arrived after
dark at the Tsar's capital. Little Fool Ivan rode to
the Palace courtyard, set down there the twenty
suckling pigs, still tied by the silken lasso,
went to the stables, and fell asleep.

In the morning the Tsar was greatly astonished
to see that Little Fool Ivan had performed the
task and was delighted to possess the new

treasure. He sent for his Master of Horse and praised him and gave him a rich present, so that the envious ones thereat were made still more envious.

So, after some days, these came to the Tsar and said, "Thy Master of Horse, O Tsar's Majesty, doth boast now that the bringing of the wonderful Pig with her twenty sucklings was but a small service, and that he could, if he but chose, bring to thee the Mare with Seven Manes and her seven fierce stallions that graze on a green meadow between the crystal hills of the Caucasus."

Then, in more anger than before, the Tsar bade them bring Little Fool Ivan to his presence and said sternly, "Heed my royal word. If in seven days thou hast not brought hither from between the crystal hills of the Caucasus the Seven-Maned Mare with her seven stallions, I will send thee where the crows shall pick thy bones!"

Little Fool Ivan went weeping to the little humpbacked horse and told him of the Tsar's new command. "Grieve not, little master," said the other; "let not thy bright head droop.

I can aid thee. Nor is this service too hard a one. Go thou to the Tsar and demand that he prepare at once a stone stable with one door opening into it and another opening out. Ask also for a horse's skin and an iron hammer of twelve poods weight."

Ivan obeyed. He demanded the stable, the horse's skin, and the iron hammer, and when all was ready the little horse said, "Lie down and sleep now, little master. The morning is wiser than the evening." Little Fool Ivan lay down and slept, and next morning at daybreak the pony waked him. Ivan tied the horse's skin to the

saddlebow, slung the hammer about his neck,
and mounted, and the little humpbacked horse
darted away like a swallow, till the dust curled
about his legs like a whirlwind. When he had
run three days and four nights without rest,
he stopped between two crystal hills and said:

"Yonder lies the green meadow whereon each
evening grazed the Mare with Seven Manes
and her seven fierce stallions. Take now thy
horse's skin and sew me within it, and presently
the mare will come and will set upon me with
her teeth. While she rends the skin from me,
do thou run and strike her between her two ears
with thy twelve-pood hammer, so that she will
be stunned. Mount me then in haste, and
thou mayst lead her after thee, and as for the
seven stallions, they will follow."

So Little Fool Ivan sewed the little horse in the
horse's skin, and when the mare with the seven
stallions came, the stallions stood afar off, but the
mare set upon him and rent the skin from him.
Then Ivan ran and struck her with the iron
hammer and stunned her, and instantly, holding
by her seven manes, leaped to the back of the
little humpbacked horse.

Scarce had he mounted, when the seven fierce stallions saw him, and came galloping after them, screaming with rage. But the little humpbacked horse was off like a dart back along the road they had come, and when they had traveled without stopping three nights and four days, they arrived at the Tsar's capital. Little Fool Ivan rode to the stone stable that had been built, went in at one door, and leaving therein the Mare with the Seven Manes, rode out of the other and barred it behind him, and the seven stallions, following the mare, were caught. Then Ivan went to his own place and went to sleep.

When they reported to the Tsar that this time also Little Fool Ivan had performed his task, the Tsar was more rejoiced than before and bestowed high rank and all manner of honors upon him, till, for hatred and malice the envious ones were beside themselves.

They conferred together and coming before the Tsar, they said, "O Tsar's Majesty! to bring the mare and the stallions, thy Master of Horse boasteth now, was but a small service, saying that, if he willed, he could fetch thee from across three times nine lands, where the little red sun rises, the beautiful Girl-Tsar, whom thou hast so long desired for thy bride, who lives on the sea-ocean in a golden boat, which she rows with silver oars."

Then was the Tsar mightily angered. "Summon this boaster again before me," he commanded, and when Little Fool Ivan was come in, he bade him bring him the lovely Girl-Tsar within twelve days or pay the forfeit with his head. So, for the third time, Ivan went weeping to the little humpbacked horse and told him the Tsar's will.

"Dry thy tears, little master," said the other, "for I can assist thee. This is not, after all, the hardest service. Go thou to the Tsar and ask for two handkerchiefs cunningly embroidered in gold, a silken tent woven with gold thread and with golden tent poles, gold and silver dishes, and all manner of wines and sweetmeats."

Ivan lost no time in obeying and when they were ready brought them to the stables. "Lie down and sleep now," said the little horse. "Tomorrow is wiser than today." Accordingly Little Fool Ivan lay down and slept till the little horse woke him at daybreak. He put all that had been prepared into a bag and mounted, and the little humpbacked horse sped away like the wind.

For six days they rode, a hundred thousand versts, till they reached a forest at the very end of the world, where the little red sun rises out of the blue sea-ocean. Here they stopped and Ivan alighted.

"Pitch now thy tent on the white sand," said the little horse. "In it spread thy embroidered handkerchiefs and on them put the wine and the gold and silver plates piled with sweetmeats. As for thee, do thou hide behind the tent and watch. From her golden boat the Girl-Tsar will see the tent and will approach it. Let her enter it and eat and drink her fill. Then go in, seize and hold her, and call for me." So saying, he ran to hide himself in the forest.

Ivan pitched the tent, prepared the food and wine, and lying down behind the tent, made a tiny hole in the silk through which to see, and waited. And before long the golden boat came sailing over the blue sea-ocean. The beautiful Girl-Tsar alighted to look at the splendid tent and, seeing the wine and sweetmeats, entered and began to eat and drink. So graceful and lovely was she that no tale could describe her and Little Fool Ivan could not gaze enough. He forgot

···

what the little horse had told him and he was still peering through the hole in the silk when the beautiful maiden sprang up, left the tent, leaped into her golden boat, and the silver oars carried her far away on the sea-ocean.

When the little humpbacked horse came running up, Ivan too late repented of his folly. "I am guilty before thee!" he said. "And now I shall never see her again!" and he began to shed tears.

"Never mind," said the little horse. "She will come again tomorrow, but if thou failest next time we must needs go back without her and thy head will be lost."

Next day Little Fool Ivan spread the wines and sweetmeats and lay down to watch as before; and again the lovely Girl-Tsar came rowing in her golden boat and entered the tent and began to regale herself. And while she ate and drank Ivan ran in and seized and held her and called to the little horse. The girl cried out and fought to be free, but when she saw how handsome Little Fool Ivan was, she quite forgot to struggle. He mounted and put her before him on the saddle, and the humpbacked horse dashed away like lightning along the road they had come.

They rode six days and on the seventh they came again to the capital, and Little Fool Ivan—with a sad heart, since he had fallen in love with her himself—brought the lovely girl to the Palace.

The Tsar was overjoyed. He came out to meet them, took the maiden by her white hand, seated her beside him beneath a silken curtain on a cushion of purple velvet, and spoke to her tender words. "O Girl-Tsar, to whom none can be compared!" he said. "My Tsaritsa that is to be! For how long have I not slept, either by night or in the white day, for thinking of thine eyes!"

But the beautiful Girl-Tsar turned from him
and would not answer and again and again
he tried his wooing, till at length she said, "O Tsar,
thou art wrinkled and gray, and hast left sixty
years behind thee, while I am but sixteen. Should
I wed thee, the Tsars of all Tsardoms would
laugh, saying that a grandfather had taken to wife
his grandchild."

Hearing this, the Tsar was angry. "It is true,"
he said, "that flowers do not bloom in winter and
that I am no longer young. But I am nevertheless
a great Tsar."

Then she replied, "I will wed no one who hath
gray hairs and who lacks teeth in his head. If
thou wilt but grow young again, then will I wed
thee right willingly."

"How can a man grow young again?" he
asked.

"There is a way, O Tsar," she said, "and it is
thus: Order three great caldrons to be placed in
thy courtyard. Fill the first with cold water,
the second with boiling water, and the third with
boiling mare's milk. He who bathes one minute
in the boiling milk, two in the boiling water,
and three in the cold water, becomes instantly

young and so handsome that it cannot be told. Do this and I will become thy Tsaritsa, but not otherwise."

The Tsar at once bade them prepare in the courtyard the three caldrons, one of cold water, one of boiling water, and one of boiling mare's milk, minded to make the test. The envious courtiers, however, came to him and said, "O Tsar's Majesty! this is a strange thing and we have never heard that a man can plunge into boiling liquid and not be scalded. We pray thee, therefore, bid thy Master of Horse bathe before thee; then mayest thou be assured that all is well." And this counsel seemed to the Tsar good and he straightaway summoned Little Fool Ivan and bade him prepare to make the trial.

When Ivan heard the Tsar's command he said to himself, "So I am to be killed like a suckling pig or a chicken!" and he went sorrowfully to the stables and told the little humpbacked horse. "Thou has found for me the Pig with the Golden Bristles," he said, "the Seven-Maned Mare, and the beautiful Girl-Tsar; but now these are all as nothing and my life is as worthless as a boot sole!" And he began to weep bitterly.

•••

"Weep not, little master," said the little horse. "This is indeed a real service that I shall serve thee. Now listen well to what I say. When thou goest to the courtyard, before thou strippest off thy clothes to bathe, ask of the Tsar to permit them to bring to thee thy little humpbacked horse, that thou mayest bid him farewell for the last time. He will agree and when I am brought there I shall gallop three times around the three kettles, dip my nose in each, and sprinkle thee. Lose not a moment then, but jump instantly in the caldron of boiling milk, then into the boiling water, and last into the cold water."

Scarcely had he instructed him when the Boyars came to bring Ivan to the courtyard. All the Court Ministers were there to see and the place was crowded with people, while the Tsar looked on from a balcony. The two caldrons were boiling hot and servants fed the great fires beneath them with heaps of fuel. Little Fool Ivan bowed low before the Tsar and prepared for the bath.

But having taken off his coat, he bowed again and said, "O Tsar's Majesty! I have but one favor to ask. Bid them bring hither my little

humpbacked horse that I may embrace him once
more for the last time!" The Tsar was in good
humor thinking he was so soon to regain his
youth, and he consented, and presently the little
horse came running into the courtyard, dancing
up and down and clapping his long ears
together. But as soon as he came to the three
caldrons he galloped three times round them,
dipped his nose into each, and sprinkled his
master; and without waiting a moment Little Fool
Ivan threw off his clothes and jumped into the
caldrons, one after the other. And while he had
been good-looking before, he came from the

last caldron so handsome that his beauty could neither be described with a pen nor written in a tale.

Now when the Tsar saw this, he could wait no longer. He hastened down from the balcony and, without waiting to undress, crossed himself and jumped into the boiling milk. But the charm did not work in his case, and he was instantly scalded to death.

Seeing the Tsar was dead, the Girl-Tsar came to the balcony and spoke to the people, saying, "Thy Tsar chose me to be his Tsaritsa. If thou wilt, I will rule this Tsardom, but it shall be only as the wife of him who brought me from mine own!"

The people, well pleased, shouted: "Health to Tsar Ivan!" And so Little Fool Ivan led the lovely Girl-Tsar to the church and they were married that same day.

Then Tsar Ivan ordered the trumpeters to blow their hammered trumpets and the butlers to open the bins, and he made in the Palace a feast like a hill, and the Boyars and Princes sat at oak tables and drank from golden goblets and made merry till they could not stand on their feet.

···

But Little Fool Ivan, with his Tsaritsa, ruled
the Tsardom wisely and well, and grew
never too wise to take counsel of his little
humpbacked horse.

OOKA AND THE HONEST THIEF

*Japanese folktale
as told by I. G. Edmonds*

One day, Yahichi, owner of a rice store, came to Ooka's court, complaining that each night some of his rice disappeared.

"It is such a small amount that I hesitate to trouble your Honorable Honor," Yahichi said, touching the ground with his head to show proper respect for the great magistrate. "But I am reminded of the story of the mountain that was reduced to a plain because a single grain was stolen from it each day for centuries."

Ooka nodded gravely. "It is just as dishonest to steal one grain of rice as it is to steal a large sack," he remarked. "Did you take proper steps to guard your property?"

"Yes, my lord. I stationed a guard with the rice each night, but still it disappears. I cannot understand it," the rice merchant said, pulling his white beard nervously.

"What about your guard. Can he be trusted?" Ooka asked.

"Absolutely, Lord Ooka," Yahichi said. "The guard is Chogoro. He has served my family for seventy-five years."

"Yes, I know Chogoro," Ooka said. "He is a most conscientious man. He could not be the thief. But it is possible that he falls asleep at his post. After all, he is eighty years old."

"A man can be just as alert at eighty as at twenty," Yahichi replied quickly. "I am eighty-one myself, and I have never been so alert. Besides, I stood guard myself with Chogoro these last two nights. The rice vanished just the same."

"In that case I will watch with you tonight," Ooka said. "I should like to see this for myself."

•••

As he had promised, Ooka made his way
that evening to Yahichi's rice store. He was sure
that both Yahichi and Chogoro had fallen asleep
and had allowed the thief to enter each time the
rice had been stolen, and it was not long before
his suspicions were proved correct. Within an
hour, both men were sleeping soundly. Ooka
smiled. He was certain that when the men
awoke neither would admit he had slept at all.

A little past midnight, Ooka heard a slight
sound outside the building. He sprang to his feet
and peered cautiously out the window. To his
astonishment, Ooka found himself staring
straight into the face of a man standing in the
shadows just outside the building. The judge
recognized him as Gonta, a laborer who had
been out of work for some time. The man
was rooted to the spot by fear.

Ooka hesitated to arrest him. After all, he had
not entered the rice store. Ooka would have no
proof that he had come to steal. He could simply
say that he had lost his way in the dark.

Though Ooka had recognized the thief, Gonta
had not recognized the judge, for the darkness
inside the building hid his face.

Ooka decided the best thing to do would be to pretend that he, too, was a thief. In this way he might trap Gonta into completing his crime. Speaking in a harsh tone to disguise his voice, he said, "You have obviously come here to steal rice just as I have."

Gonta was relieved to find himself face to face with another thief instead of a guard.

"As a favor from one thief to another," Ooka continued, "I will pass the rice out to you, so that you will not need to risk coming in yourself."

Gonta thanked him profusely for his courtesy, and Ooka picked up a large sack of rice and handed it out to him.

"This is too much," Gonta protested. "I want only a few handfuls."

Ooka was amazed. "But if you are going to steal, you may as well take a large amount. After all, if Ooka catches you, you will be punished as much for stealing a single grain as you would for a whole sack."

"That would be dishonest!" Gonta replied indignantly. "I take just enough to feed my family for a single day, for each day I hope I will find work and not have to steal anymore. If I do find work, I intend to return all I have taken."

Then he took out the amount of rice he needed for his family's daily meal and handed the sack back to the astonished judge. Thanking Ooka once more for his courtesy, Gonta turned and disappeared into the darkness. Ooka did not try to stop him.

When the shopkeeper and his guard awoke, Ooka told them what had happened.

"But why did you let the thief go?" Yahichi asked indignantly.

"Gonta is certainly a thief," Ooka replied. "But I am convinced he is an honest one, for he refused to steal more than he needed."

"But, Lord Ooka, how can a man be a thief and honest at the same time?"

"I would never have believed it possible, but it is so," Ooka said. "It is the duty of a judge to punish wickedness and reward virtue. In this case, we find both qualities in the same man, so obviously it would be unfair to treat him as any ordinary thief."

"But, Lord Ooka—"

"I have made my decision. Tomorrow I will see that work is found for Gonta which is sufficient to feed his family and still leave enough to allow him to pay back the rice he stole. We will see if he keeps his promise. If he returns here and replaces the extra amount each night, it will prove my belief that he is an honest thief."

The plan was carried out according to Ooka's wishes. Gonta was given a job, without knowing that Ooka was responsible. And, as the judge suspected, every night Gonta took the rice left over from his day's earnings and left it in the rice shop.

Ooka put all kinds of obstacles in his way to make it difficult for him to enter the shop, but this did not prevent Gonta from returning each night, although he became more and more afraid of being caught.

Yahichi admitted that the thief had been punished enough for his crime and told Ooka he did not wish to press charges. The great judge smiled and wrote out a small scroll which he ordered Yahichi to leave for Gonta to see when he came to pay for the last portion of rice.

When the honest thief slipped fearfully into the rice shop for the last time, he was shocked to find the scroll on which was written in Ooka's own handwriting, and bearing Ooka's signature, the following message:

You owe an extra ten percent for interest.
Honesty is the best policy.

THE BRAVE LITTLE TAILOR

Brothers Grimm

One summer morning a little tailor was sitting on his table near the window. He was in high good humor and sewed with all his might.

A peasant woman came down the street, crying out: "Good jam—cheap! Good jam—cheap!" That sounded sweet to the tailor's ears. He stuck his shapely little head out of the window and cried: "Up here, my good woman, you'll find a buyer."

The woman hauled her heavy baskets up the three flights of stairs to the tailor's, and he made her unpack every single pot. He examined them

all, lifted them up, sniffed at them, and finally
said: "This looks like good jam to me. Weigh me
out three ounces, my good woman, and if
it comes to a quarter of a pound you won't find
me complaining." The woman, who had
hoped to make a good sale, gave him what he
asked for, and went away grumbling and
very much out of sorts.

"God bless this jam and give
me health and strength," cried the
little tailor. Whereupon he took
bread from the cupboard, cut a
slice straight across the loaf, and
spread it with
jam. "I bet
this won't
taste bitter,"
he said, "but
before biting
into it I'm going to finish my jacket."

He put the bread down beside him and went
on with his sewing, taking bigger and bigger
stitches in his joy. Meanwhile, the flies that had
been sitting on the wall, enticed by the sweet
smell, came swarming down on the jam.

•••

"Hey, who invited you?" cried the little tailor and shooed the unbidden guests away. But the flies, who didn't understand his language, refused to be dismissed and kept coming in greater and greater numbers. Finally, at the end of his patience, the tailor took a rag from the catchall under his table. "Just wait! I'll show you!" he cried and struck out at them unmercifully. When he stopped and counted, no less than seven flies lay dead with their legs in the air.

He couldn't help admiring his bravery. "What a man I am!" he cried. "The whole town must hear of this." And one two three, he cut out a belt for himself, stitched it up, and embroidered on it in big letters: "Seven at one blow!" Then he said: "Town, my foot! The whole world must hear of it!" And for joy his heart wagged like a lamb's tail.

The tailor put on his belt and decided to go out into the world, for clearly his shop was too small for such valor. Before leaving, he ransacked the house for something to take with him, but all he could find was an old cheese, so he put that in his pocket. Just outside the door, he caught sight of a bird that had got itself caught in the bushes, and the bird joined the cheese in his pocket. Ever so bravely he took to the road, and because he was light and nimble, he never seemed to get tired.

Up into the mountains he went, and when he reached the highest peak he found an enormous giant sitting there taking it easy and enjoying the view. The little tailor went right up to him. He wasn't the least bit afraid. "Greetings, friend," he said. "Looking out at the great world, are you? Well, that's just where I'm headed for, to try my luck. Would you care to go with me?"

The giant looked at the tailor contemptuously and said: "You little pipsqueak! You miserable nobody!"

"Is that so?" said the little tailor, unbuttoning his coat and showing the giant his belt. "Read that! That'll show you the kind of man I am!"

When he had read what was written—"Seven at one blow!"—the giant thought somewhat better of the little man. All the same, he decided to put him to the test, so he picked up a stone and squeezed it until drops of water appeared. "Do that," he said, "if you've got the strength."

"That?" said the tailor. "Why, that's child's play for a man like me." Whereupon he reached into his pocket, took out the soft cheese, and squeezed it until the whey ran out. "What do you think of that?" he cried. "Not so bad, eh?"

The giant didn't know what to say. He couldn't believe the little man was so strong. So he picked up a stone and threw it so high that the eye could hardly keep up with it. "All right, you little runt, let's see you do that."

"Nice throw," said the tailor, "but it fell to the ground in the end. Watch me throw one that won't ever come back." Whereupon he reached into his pocket, took out the bird, and tossed it into the air. Glad to be free, the bird flew up and away

and didn't come back. "Well," said the tailor.
"What do you think of that?"

"I've got to admit you can throw," said
the giant, "but now let's see what you can carry."
Pointing at a big oak tree that lay felled on
the ground, he said: "If you're strong enough,
help me carry this tree out of the forest."

"Glad to," said the little man. "You take
the trunk over your shoulder, and I'll carry the
branches; they're the heaviest part."

The giant took the trunk over his shoulder,
and the tailor sat down on a branch,
so that the giant, who couldn't

look around, had to carry the whole tree and
the tailor to boot. The tailor felt so chipper
in his comfortable back seat that he began to
whistle "Three Tailors Went a-Riding," as though
hauling trees were child's play to a man of
his strength.

After carrying the heavy load for quite some
distance, the giant was exhausted. "Hey!" he
cried out, "I've got to drop it." The tailor jumped
nimbly down, put his arms around the tree as if
he'd been carrying it, and said to the giant:
"I wouldn't have thought a tiny tree would be
too much for a big man like you."

They went on together until they came to a
cherry tree. The giant grabbed the crown where
the cherries ripen soonest, pulled it down,
handed it to the tailor, and bade him eat. But the
tailor was much too light to hold the tree down.
When the giant let go, the crown snapped
back into place and the tailor was whisked high
into the air. When he had fallen to the ground
without hurting himself, the giant cried out:
"What's the matter? You mean you're not strong
enough to hold that bit of a sapling?"

"Not strong enough? How can you say such a thing about a man who did for seven at one blow? I jumped over that tree because the hunters down there were shooting into the thicket. Now you try. See if you can do it."

The giant tried, but he couldn't get over the tree and got stuck in the upper branches. Once again the little tailor had won out.

"All right," said the giant. "If you're so brave, let me take you to our cave to spend the night with us."

The little tailor was willing and went along with him. When they got to the cave, the other giants were sitting around the fire. Each one was holding a roasted sheep in his hands and eating it. The little tailor looked around and thought: "This place is a good deal roomier than my workshop."

The giant showed him a bed and told him to lie down and sleep. But the bed was too big for the little tailor, so instead of getting into it, he crept into a corner. At midnight, when the giant thought the tailor must be sound asleep, he got up, took a big iron bar and split the bed

in two with one stroke. That will settle the little runt's hash, he thought.

At the crack of dawn the giants started into the forest. They had forgotten all about the little tailor. All at once he came striding along as chipper and bold as you please. The giants were terrified. They thought he would kill them all, and ran away as fast as their legs would carry them.

The little tailor went his way. After following his nose for many days he came to the grounds

of a king's palace. Feeling tired, he lay down
in the grass and went to sleep, and while he
was sleeping some courtiers came along.
They examined him from all sides and read the
inscription on his belt: "Seven at one blow!"

"Goodness," they said, "what can a great war
hero like this be doing here in peacetime?
He must be some great lord." They went and
told the king. "If war should break out," they
said, "a man like that would come in very handy.
Don't let him leave on any account."

This struck the king as good advice, and he
sent one of his courtiers to offer the tailor a post
in his army. The courtier went back to the
sleeper, waited until he stretched his limbs and
opened his eyes, and made his offer. "That's just
what I came here for," said the tailor. "I'll be glad
to enter the king's service." So he was received
with honor and given apartments of his own.

But the soldiers, who were taken in by the
little tailor, wished him a thousand miles away.
"What will become of us?" they asked. "If we
quarrel with him and he strikes, seven of us will
fall at one blow. We won't last long at that rate."
So they took counsel together, went to the king,

and asked to be released from his service.
"Because," they said, "we can't hope to
keep up with a man who does for
seven at one blow."

The king was sad to be losing all his faithful
servants because of one and wished he had
never laid eyes on him. He'd have been glad to
get rid of him, but he didn't dare dismiss him for
fear the great hero might strike him and all his
people dead and seize the throne for himself.

He thought and thought, and at last he hit on
an idea. He sent word to the little tailor that since
he was such a great hero he wanted to make

him an offer. There were two giants living in a
certain forest, and they were murdering, looting,
burning, and laying the country waste. No one
dared go near them for fear of his life. If the
hero should conquer and kill these two giants,
the king would give him his only daughter to
wife, with half his kingdom as her dowry.
And, moreover, the king would send a hundred
knights to back him up.

"Sounds like just the thing for me," thought
the little tailor. "It's not every day that somebody
offers you a beautiful princess and half a
kingdom."

"It's a deal," he replied. "I'll take care of those
giants, and I won't need the hundred knights.
You can't expect a man who does for seven at
one blow to be afraid of two."

The little tailor started out with the hundred
knights at his heels. When they got to the
edge of the forest, he said to his companions:
"Stay here. I'll attend to the giants by myself."
Then he bounded into the woods, peering
to the right and to the left.

After a while he caught sight of the two giants,
who were lying under a tree asleep, snoring so

hard that the
branches rose
and fell. Quick as
a flash the little
tailor picked up
stones, filled both
his pockets with
them, and climbed
the tree. Halfway up,
he slid along a branch
until he was right over
the sleeping giants.
Then he picked out
one of the giants and
dropped stone after
stone on his chest.

For a long while the giant didn't notice,
but in the end he woke up, gave his companion
a poke, and said: "Why are you hitting me?"

"You're dreaming," said the other. "I'm not
hitting you."

When they had lain down to sleep again,
the tailor dropped a stone on the second
giant. "What is this?" he cried. "Why are you
pelting me?"

"I'm not pelting you!"
the first grumbled.
They argued awhile,
but they were too tired
to keep it up and finally
their eyes closed again.
Then the little tailor took
his biggest stone and
threw it with all his might
at the first giant's chest.
"This is too much!" cried the
giant and, jumping up
like a madman, he
pushed his companion
so hard against the tree that it shook. The other
repaid him in kind, and they both flew into
such a rage that they started pulling up trees
and belaboring each other until they both
lay dead on the ground.

The little tailor jumped down. "Lucky they
didn't pull up the tree I was sitting in," he said to
himself. "I'd have had to jump into another like
a squirrel. But then we tailors are quick."

He drew his sword, gave them both good
thrusts in the chest, and went back to the

knights. "The job is done," he said. "I've settled their hash. But it was a hard fight. They were so desperate they pulled up trees to fight with, but how could that help them against a man who does for seven at one blow!"

"Aren't you even wounded?" the knights asked.

"I should say not!" said the tailor. "Not so much as a scratch."

The knights wouldn't believe him, so they rode into the forest, where they found the giants lying in pools of blood, with uprooted trees all around them.

The little tailor went to the king and demanded the promised reward, but the king regretted his promise and thought up another way to get rid of the hero. "Before I give you my daughter and half my kingdom," he said, "you will have to perform one more task. There's a unicorn loose in the forest and he's doing a good deal of damage. You will have to catch him first."

"If the two giants didn't scare me, why would I worry about a unicorn? Seven at one blow is my meat." Taking a rope and an ax, he went into

the forest and again told the knights who had
been sent with him to wait on the fringe.

He didn't have long to look. In a short while
the unicorn came along and rushed at the tailor,
meaning to run him straight through with his
horn. "Not so fast!" said the tailor. "It's not
as easy as all that." He stood still, waited until
the unicorn was quite near him, and then
jumped nimbly behind a tree.

The unicorn charged full force and rammed
into the tree. His horn went in and stuck
so fast that he hadn't the
strength to pull it out.
He was caught.

"I've got him," said the tailor. He came out from behind the tree, put the rope around the unicorn's neck, and, taking his ax, chopped the wood away from the horn. When that was done, he led the beast to the king.

But the king was still unwilling to grant him the promised reward and made a third demand. Before the wedding he wanted the tailor to capture a wild boar which had been ravaging the forest, and said the royal huntsmen would help him.

"Gladly," said the little tailor. "It's child's play." He didn't take the huntsmen into the forest with him, and they were just as pleased, for several times the boar had given them such a reception that they had no desire to seek him out.

When the boar caught sight of the tailor, he gnashed his teeth, foamed at the mouth, made a dash at him, and would have lain him out flat if the nimble hero hadn't escaped into a nearby chapel. The boar ran in after him, but the tailor jumped out of the window, ran around the chapel, and slammed the door. The infuriated beast was much too heavy and clumsy to jump out of the window, and so he was caught.

The little tailor ran back to the huntsmen and told them to go and see the captive with their own eyes. He himself went to the king, who had to keep his promise this time, like it or not, and give him his daughter and half the kingdom. If he had known that, far from being a war hero, the bridegroom was only a little tailor, he would have been even unhappier than he was. And so the wedding was celebrated with great splendor and little joy, and a tailor became a king.

One night the young queen heard her husband talking in his sleep. "Boy," he said, "hurry up with that jerkin you're making and get those breeches mended, or I'll break my yardstick over your head." Then she knew how he had got his start in life. Next morning she went to her father, told him her tale of woe, and begged him to help her get rid of a husband who had turned out to be a common tailor.

The king bade her take comfort and said: "Leave the door of your bedroom unlocked tonight. My servants will be waiting outside. Once he's asleep they'll go in, tie him up, and put him aboard a ship bound for the end of the world."

The young queen was pleased, but the armor-bearer, who was devoted to the hero, heard the whole conversation and told him all about the plot. "They won't get away with that!" said the little tailor.

That night he went to bed with his wife at the usual hour. When she thought he was asleep, she got up, opened the door, and lay down again. The little tailor, who was only pretending to be asleep, cried out in a loud voice: "Boy, hurry up with that jerkin you're making and get those breeches mended, or I'll break my yardstick over your head. I've done for seven at one blow, killed two giants, brought home a unicorn, and captured a wild boar. And now I'm expected to be afraid of these scoundrels at my door."

When they heard that, the servants were terrified. Not one of them dared lay hands on him, and they ran as if the hosts of hell had been chasing them. And so the little tailor went on being a king for the rest of his days.

*   *Jean Labadie was the most popular storyteller.*   *

JEAN LABADIE'S BIG BLACK DOG

French-Canadian folktale
as told by Natalie Savage Carlson

Once in another time, Jean Labadie was the most popular storyteller in the parish. He acted out every story so that it would seem more real.

When he told about the great falls in Niagara, he made a booming noise deep in his throat and whirled his fists around each other. Then each listener could plainly hear the falls and see the white water churning and splashing as if it were about to pour down on his own head. But Jean Labadie had to stop telling his stories about the *loup-garou,* the demon who takes the shape of a terrible animal and pounces upon those foolish people who go out alone at night.

...

Every time the storyteller dropped down on all fours, rolled his eyes, snorted, and clawed at the floor, his listeners ran away from him in terror.

It was only on the long winter evenings that Jean had time to tell these tales. All the rest of the year, he worked hard with his cows and his pigs and his chickens.

One day Jean Labadie noticed that his flock of chickens was getting smaller and smaller. He began to suspect that his neighbor, André Drouillard, was stealing them. Yet he never could catch André in the act.

For three nights running, Jean took his gun down from the wall and slept in the henhouse with his chickens. But the only thing that happened was that his hens were disturbed by having their feeder roost with them, and they stopped laying well. So Jean sighed and put his gun back and climbed into his own bed again.

One afternoon when Jean went to help his neighbor mow the weeds around his barn, he found a bunch of gray chicken feathers near

the fence. Now he was sure that André was
taking his chickens, for all of his neighbor's
chickens were scrawny white things.

He did not know how to broach the matter to
André without making an enemy of him. And
when one lives in the country and needs help
with many tasks, it is a great mistake to make an
enemy of a close neighbor. Jean studied the
matter as his scythe went swish, swish through
the tall weeds. At last he thought of a way out.

"Have you seen my big black dog, André?"
he asked his neighbor.

"What big black dog?" asked André. "I didn't know you had a dog."

"I just got him from the Indians," said Jean. "Someone has been stealing my chickens so I got myself a dog to protect them. He is a very fierce dog, bigger than a wolf and twice as wild."

Jean took one hand off the scythe and pointed to the ridge behind the barn.

"There he goes now," he cried, "with his big red tongue hanging out of his mouth. See him!"

André looked but could see nothing.

"Surely you must see him. He runs along so fast. He lifts one paw this way and another paw that way."

As Jean said this, he dropped the scythe and lifted first one hand in its black glove and then the other.

···

André looked at the black gloves going up and down like the paws of a big black dog. Then he looked toward the ridge. He grew excited.

"Yes, yes," he cried, "I do see him now. He is running along the fence. He lifts one paw this way and another paw that way, just like you say."

Jean was pleased that he was such a good actor he could make André see a dog that didn't exist at all.

"Now that you have seen him," he said, "you will know him if you should meet. Give him a wide path and don't do anything that will make him suspicious. He is a very fierce watchdog."

André promised to stay a safe distance from the big black dog.

Jean Labadie was proud of himself over the success of his trick. No more chickens disappeared. It seemed that his problem was solved.

Then one day André greeted him with, "I saw your big black dog in the road today. He was running along lifting one paw this way and another paw that way. I got out of his way, you can bet my life!"

Jean Labadie was pleased and annoyed at the same time. Pleased that André believed so completely in the big black dog that he could actually see him. He was also annoyed because the big black dog had been running down the road when he should have been on the farm.

Another day André leaned over the fence.

"Good day, Jean Labadie," he said. "I saw your big black dog on the other side of the village. He was jumping over fences and bushes. Isn't it a bad thing for him to wander so far away? Someone might take him for the *loup-garou*."

Jean Labadie was disgusted with his neighbor's good imagination.

"André," he asked, "how can my dog be on the other side of the village when he is right here at home? See him walking through the yard, lifting one paw this way and another paw that way?"

André looked in Jean's yard with surprise.

"And so he is," he agreed. "My faith, what a one he is! He must run like lightning to get home so fast. Perhaps you should chain him up. Someone will surely mistake such a fast dog for the *loup-garou*."

Jean shrugged hopelessly.

"All right," he said, "perhaps you are right.
I will chain him near the henhouse."

"They will be very happy to hear that in the
village," said André. "Everyone is afraid of him.
I have told them all about him, how big
and fierce he is, how his long red
tongue hangs out of his mouth, and
how he lifts one paw this way
and another paw that way."

Jean was angry.

"I would thank you to leave
my dog alone, André Drouillard,"
he said stiffly.

"Oh, ho, and that I do,"
retorted André.
"But today on the
road he growled
and snapped at me.
I would not be
here to tell
the story if I
hadn't taken
to a tall
maple tree."

Jean Labadie pressed his lips together.

"Then I will chain him up this very moment." He gave a long low whistle. "Come, fellow! Here, fellow!"

André took to his heels.

Of course, this should have ended the matter, and Jean Labadie thought that it had. But one day when he went to the village to buy some nails for his roof, he ran into Madame Villeneuve in a great how-does-it-make of excitement.

"Jean Labadie," she cried to him, "you should be ashamed of yourself, letting that fierce dog run loose in the village."

"But my dog is chained up in the yard at home," said Jean.

"So André Drouillard told me," said Madame, "but he has broken loose. He is running along lifting one paw this way and another paw that way, with the broken chain dragging in the dust. He growled at me and bared his fangs. It's a lucky thing his chain caught on a bush or I would not be talking to you now."

Jean sighed.

"Perhaps I should get rid of my big black dog," he said. "Tomorrow I will take him back to the Indians."

So next day Jean hitched his horse to the cart
and waited until he saw André Drouillard at
work in his garden. Then he whistled loudly
toward the yard, made a great show of helping
his dog climb up between the wheels and drove
past André's house with one arm curved out in
a bow, as if it were around the dog's neck.

"*Au revoir,* André!" he called. Then he looked
at the empty half of the seat. "Bark goodbye
to André Drouillard, fellow, for you are leaving
here forever."

Jean drove out to the Indian village and spent
the day with his friends, eating and talking.
It seemed a bad waste of time when there was
so much to be done on the farm,
but on the other hand,

it was worth idling all day in order to end the big black dog matter.

Dusk was falling as he rounded the curve near his home. He saw the shadowy figure of André Drouillard waiting for him near his gate. A feeling of foreboding came over Jean.

"What is it?" he asked his neighbor. "Do you have some bad news for me?"

"It's about your big black dog," said André. "He has come back home. Indeed he beat you by an hour. It was that long ago I saw him running down the road to your house with his big red tongue hanging out of his mouth and lifting one paw this way and another paw that way."

Jean was filled with rage. For a twist of tobacco, he would have struck André with his horsewhip.

"André Drouillard," he shouted, "you are a liar! I just left the big black dog with the Indians. They have tied him up."

André sneered.

"A liar am I? We shall see who is the liar. Wait until the others see your big black dog running around again."

•••

So Jean might as well have accused André
of being a chicken thief in the first place,
for now they were enemies anyway. And he
certainly might as well have stayed home
and fixed his roof.

Things turned out as his neighbor had hinted.
Madame Villeneuve saw the big black dog
running behind her house. Henri Dupuis saw
him running around the corner of the store.
Delphine Langlois even saw him running
through the graveyard among the tombstones.
And always as he ran along, he lifted one
paw this way and another paw that way.

There came that day when Jean Labadie left
his neighbor chopping wood all by himself,
because they were no longer friends, and drove
into the village to have his black mare shod.
While he was sitting in front of the
blacksmith shop, André Drouillard
came galloping up at a great speed.
He could scarcely hold the reins,
for one hand was cut and
bleeding.

A crowd quickly gathered.
"What is wrong, André
Drouillard?" they asked.
"Have you cut yourself?"
"Where is Dr. Brisson?
Someone fetch Dr. Brisson."
André Drouillard pointed
his bleeding hand at Jean
Labadie.
"His big black dog bit me,"
he accused. "Without warning,
he jumped the fence as soon as Jean drove
away and sank his teeth into my hand."
There was a gasp of horror from every throat.
Jean Labadie reddened. He walked over to
André and stared at the wound.

"It looks like an ax cut to me," he said.

Then everyone grew angry at Jean Labadie and his big black dog. They threatened to drive them both out of the parish.

"My friends," said Jean wearily, "I think it is time for this matter to be ended. The truth of it is that I have no big black dog. I never had a big black dog. It was all a joke."

"Aha!" cried André. "Now he is trying to crawl out of the blame. He says he has no big black dog. Yet I have seen it with my own eyes, running around and lifting one paw this way and another paw that way."

"I have seen it, too," cried Madame Villeneuve. "It ran up and growled at me."

"And I."

"And I."

Jean Labadie bowed his head.

"All right, my friends," he said. "There is nothing more I can do about it. I guess that big black dog will eat me out of house and home for the rest of my life."

"You mean you won't make things right about this hand?" demanded André Drouillard.

"What do you want me to do?" asked Jean.

175

"I will be laid up for a week at least," said André Drouillard, "and right at harvest time. Then, too, there may be a scar. But for two of your plumpest pullets, I am willing to overlook the matter and be friends again."

"That is fair," cried Henri Dupuis.

"It is just," cried the blacksmith.

"A generous proposal," agreed everyone.

"And now we will return to my farm," said Jean Labadie, "and I will give André two of my pullets. But all of you must come. I want witnesses."

A crowd trooped down the road to watch the transaction.

After Jean had given his neighbor two of his best pullets, he commanded the crowd, "Wait!"

He went into the house. When he returned, he was carrying his gun.

"I want witnesses," explained Jean, "because I am going to shoot my big black dog. I want everyone to see this happen."

The crowd murmured and surged. Jean gave a long low whistle toward the henhouse.

"Here comes my big black dog," he pointed.

"You can see how he runs to me with his big
red tongue hanging out and lifting one paw this
way and another paw that way."

Everyone saw the big black dog.

Jean Labadie lifted his gun to his shoulder,
pointed it at nothing and pulled the trigger. There
was a deafening roar and the gun kicked Jean to
the ground. He arose and brushed off his blouse.
Madame Villeneuve screamed and Delphine
Langlois fainted.

"There," said Jean, brushing away a tear,
"it is done. That is the end of my big black dog.
Isn't that true?"

And everyone agreed that the dog was gone
for good.

CAPORUSHES

English folktale
as told by Flora Annie Steel

Once upon a time, a long, long while ago, when all the world was young and all sorts of strange things happened, there lived a very rich gentleman whose wife had died, leaving him three lovely daughters. They were as the apple of his eye, and he loved them exceedingly.

Now one day he wanted to find out if they loved him in return, so he said to the eldest, "How much do you love me, my dear?"

And she answered as pat as may be, "As I love my life."

"Very good, my dear," said he, and gave her a kiss. Then he said to the second girl, "How much do you love me, my dear?"

And she answered as swift as thought, "Better than all the world beside."

"Good!" he replied, and patted her on the cheek. Then he turned to the youngest, who was also the prettiest.

"And how much do *you* love me, my dearest?"

Now the youngest daughter was not only pretty, she was clever. So she thought a moment, then she said slowly: "I love you as fresh meat loves salt!"

Now when her father heard this he was very angry, because he really loved her more than the others.

"What!" he said. "If that is all you give me in return for all I've given you, out of my house you go." So there and then he turned her out of the home where she had been born and bred, and shut the door in her face.

Not knowing where to go, she wandered on, and she wandered on, till she came to a big fen where the reeds grew ever so tall and the rushes swayed in the wind like a field of corn.

•••

There she sat down and plaited herself an overall of rushes and a cap to match, so as to hide her fine clothes and her beautiful golden hair that was all set with milk-white pearls. For she was a wise girl and thought that in such lonely country, mayhap, some robber might fall in with her and kill her to get her fine clothes and jewels.

It took a long time to plait the dress and cap, and while she plaited she sang a little song:

> Hide my hair, O cap o' rushes,
> Hide my heart, O robe o' rushes.
> Sure! my answer had no fault
> I love him more than he loves salt.

And the fen birds sat and listened and sang back to her:

> Cap o' rushes, shed no tear,
> Robe o' rushes, have no fear.
> With these words if fault he'd find,
> Sure your father must be blind.

When her task was finished she put on her robe of rushes, and it hid all her fine clothes. And she put on the cap, and it hid all her beautiful hair, so that she looked quite a common country girl. But the fen birds flew away, singing as they flew:

Cap o' rushes! we can see,
Robe o' rushes! what you be,
Fair and clean, and fine and tidy,
So you'll be whate'er betide ye.

By this time she was very, very hungry, so she wandered on, and she wandered on. But ne'er a cottage or a hamlet did she see, till just at sunsetting she came on a great house on the

edge of the fen. It had a fine front door to it, but mindful of her dress of rushes she went round to the back. And there she saw a strapping fat scullion washing pots and pans with a very sulky face. So, being a clever girl, she guessed what the maid was wanting and said: "If I may have a night's lodging, I will scrub the pots and pans for you."

"Why! Here's luck," replied the scullery maid, ever so pleased. "I was just wanting badly to go walking with my sweetheart. So if you will do my work you shall share my bed and have a bite of my supper. Only mind you scrub the pots clean, or Cook will be at me."

Now next morning the pots were scraped so clean that they looked like new, and the saucepans were polished like silver, and the cook said to the scullion, "Who cleaned these pots? Not you, I'll swear." So the maid had to up and out with the truth. Then the cook would have turned away the old maid and put on the new, but the latter would not hear of it.

"The maid was kind to me and gave me a night's lodging," she said. "So now I will stay without wages and do the dirty work for her."

So Caporushes—for so they called her since she would give no other name—stayed on and cleaned the pots and scraped the saucepans.

Now it so happened that her master's son came of age, and to celebrate the occasion a ball

was given to the neighbourhood, for the young
man was a grand dancer and loved nothing so
well as a country measure. It was a very fine
party, and after supper was served, the servants
were allowed to go and watch the quality
from the gallery of the ballroom.

But Caporushes refused to go, for she also was
a grand dancer, and she was afraid that when
she heard the fiddles starting a merry jig, she
might start dancing. So she excused herself by
saying she was too tired with scraping pots
and washing saucepans, and when the others
went off she crept up to her bed.

But alas! and alack-a-day! The door had been
left open, and as she lay in her bed she could
hear the fiddlers fiddling
away and the tramp
of dancing feet.

Then she
upped and off
with her cap
and robe of
rushes, and there
she was, ever
so fine and tidy.

She was in the ballroom in a trice, joining in the jig, and none was more beautiful or better dressed than she. While as for her dancing . . . !

Her master's son singled her out at once and with the finest of bows engaged her as his partner for the rest of the night. So she danced away to her heart's content, while the whole room was agog, trying to find out who the beautiful young stranger could be. But she kept her own counsel and, making some excuse, slipped away before the ball finished. So when her fellow servants came to bed, there she was in hers, in her cap and robe of rushes, pretending to be fast asleep.

Next morning, however, the maids could talk of nothing but the beautiful stranger.

•••

"You should have seen her," they said. "She was the loveliest young lady as ever you see, not a bit like the likes o' we. Her golden hair was all silvered with pearls, and her dress—law! You wouldn't believe how she was dressed. Young master never took his eyes off her."

And Caporushes only smiled and said, with a twinkle in her eye, "I should like to see her, but I don't think I ever shall."

"Oh, yes, you will," they replied, "for young master has ordered another ball tonight in hopes she will come to dance again."

But that evening Caporushes refused once more to go to the gallery, saying she was too tired with cleaning pots and scraping saucepans. And once more when she heard the fiddlers fiddling she said to herself, "I must have one dance—just one with the young master: he dances so beautifully." For she felt certain he would dance with her.

And sure enough, when she had upped and offed with her cap and robe of rushes, there he was at the door waiting for her to come. For he had determined to dance with no one else.

So he took her by the hand, and they danced down the ballroom. It was a sight of all sights! Never were such dancers! So young, so handsome, so fine, so gay!

But once again Caporushes kept her own counsel and just slipped away on some excuse in time, so that when her fellow servants came to their beds they found her in hers, pretending to be fast asleep; but her cheeks were all flushed and her breath came fast. So they said, "She is dreaming. We hope her dreams are happy."

But next morning they were full of what she had missed. Never was such a beautiful young gentleman as young master! Never was such a beautiful young lady! Never was such beautiful dancing! Everyone else had stopped theirs to look on.

And Caporushes, with a twinkle in her eyes, said, "I should like to see her, but I'm *sure* I never shall!"

"Oh yes!" they replied. "If you come tonight you're sure to see her, for young master has ordered another ball in hopes the beautiful stranger will come again. For it's easy to see he is madly in love with her."

Then Caporushes told herself she would not dance again, since it was not fit for a gay young master to be in love with his scullery maid. But, alas! the moment she heard the fiddlers fiddling, she just upped and offed with her rushes, and there she was, fine and tidy as ever! She didn't even have to brush her beautiful golden hair!

And once again she was in the ballroom in a trice, dancing away with young master, who never took his eyes off her and implored her to tell him who she was. But she kept her own counsel and only told him that she never, never, never would come to dance anymore, and that he must say goodbye. And he held her hand so fast that she had a job to get away, and lo and behold! his ring came off his finger, and as she ran up to her bed there it was in her hand! She had just time to put on her cap and robe of rushes, when her fellow servants came trooping in and found her awake.

"It was the noise you made coming upstairs," she made excuse. But they said, "Not we! It is the whole place that is in an uproar searching for the beautiful stranger. Young master he tried to detain her, but she slipped from him like an eel. But he declares he will find her, for if he doesn't he will die of love for her."

Then Caporushes laughed. "Young men don't die of love," said she. "He will find someone else."

But he didn't. He spent his whole time looking for his beautiful dancer, but go where he might, and ask whom he would, he never heard anything about her. And day by day he grew thinner and thinner, and paler and paler, until at last he took to his bed.

And the housekeeper came to the cook and said, "Cook the nicest dinner you can cook, for young master eats nothing."

Then the cook prepared soups and jellies and creams and roast chicken and bread sauce, but the young man would none of them.

And Caporushes cleaned the pots and scraped the saucepans and said nothing.

Then the housekeeper came crying and said to the cook, "Prepare some gruel for young master. Mayhap he'd take that. If not he will die for love of the beautiful dancer. If she could see him now, she would have pity on him."

So the cook began to make the gruel, and Caporushes left scraping saucepans and watched her.

"Let me stir it," she said, "while you fetch a cup from the pantry room."

So Caporushes stirred the gruel, and what did she do but slip young master's ring into it before the cook came back!

Then the butler took the cup upstairs on a silver salver. But when the young master saw it he waved it away, till the butler, with tears, begged him just to taste it.

So the young master took a silver spoon and stirred the gruel, and he felt something hard at the bottom of the cup. And when he fished it

up, lo! it was his own ring! Then he sat up in
bed and said quite loud, "Send for the cook!"

And when she came he asked her who made
the gruel.

"I did," she said, for she was half-pleased and
half-frightened.

Then he looked at her all over and said,
"No, you didn't! You're too stout! Tell me who
made it and you shan't be harmed!"

Then the cook began to cry. "If you please,
sir, I *did* make it. But Caporushes stirred it."

"And who is Caporushes?" asked the young
man.

"If you please, sir, Caporushes is the scullion," whimpered the cook.

Then the young man sighed and fell back on his pillow. "Send Caporushes here," he said in a faint voice, for he really was very near dying.

And when Caporushes came he just looked at her cap and her robe of rushes and turned his face to the wall. But he asked her in a weak little voice, "From whom did you get that ring?"

Now when Caporushes saw the poor young man so weak and worn with love for her, her heart melted, and she replied softly: "From him that gave it me," and offed with her cap and robe of rushes. And there she was as fine and tidy as ever, with her beautiful golden hair all silvered over with pearls.

And the young man caught sight of her with the tail of his eye, and sat up in bed as strong as may be, and drew her to him and gave her a great big kiss. So, of course, they were to be married in spite of her being only a scullery maid, for she told no one who she was.

Now everyone far and near was asked to the wedding. Among the invited guests was Caporushes' father, who from grief at losing his favourite daughter had lost his sight and was very dull and miserable. However, as a friend of the family, he had to come to the young master's wedding.

Now the marriage feast was to be the finest ever seen. But Caporushes went to her friend the cook and said: "Dress every dish without one mite of salt."

"That'll be rare and nasty," replied the cook. But because she prided herself on having let Caporushes stir the gruel and so saved the young master's life, she did as she was asked and dressed every dish for the wedding breakfast without one mite of salt.

Now when the company sat down to table their faces were full of smiles and content, for all the dishes looked so nice and tasty. But no sooner had the guests begun to eat than their faces fell, for nothing can be tasty without salt.

Then Caporushes' blind father, whom his daughter had seated next to her, burst out crying.

"What is the matter?" she asked.

Then the old man sobbed, "I had a daughter whom I loved dearly, dearly. And I asked her how much she loved me, and she replied,

'As fresh meat loves salt.' And I was angry with her and turned her out of house and home, for I thought she didn't love me at all. But now I see she loved me best of all."

And as he said the words his eyes were opened, and there beside him was his daughter, lovelier than ever.

And she gave him one hand, and her husband the young master the other, and laughed, saying, "I love you both as fresh meat loves salt." And after that they were all happy for evermore.

IT'S ALL THE FAULT OF ADAM

Nigerian folktale
as told by Barbara Walker

Long ago and far away there
was a poor woodcutter named
Iyapò. This Iyapò lived in the
smallest hut of his village, and if he
had been lazy he would have gone
hungry to his mat at night.

But every morning he arose very early and
went out well beyond his village to the forest.
There the whole morning long he cut wood,
good hard wood to make hot cooking fires. As
soon as the sun shone high overhead, Iyapò
loaded the wood on his shoulders and walked

back along the highway and through the town gate, giving a few dry sticks to the gateman for his toll. Never mind how hungry he was. He must sell his firewood before he could buy even so much as a yam for his dinner.

"Wood! Wood!" he called as he walked up and down the winding streets. "It's all the fault of Adam. Wood! Good wood for sale!" And every day somehow he managed to sell his wood.

One day as Iyapò stopped in the market to cry, "Wood! Good wood for sale!" the *oba*, the king of the town, happened to hear him.

"Who is that man?" the king asked the *otun*, his chief adviser. "And what does he mean by saying, 'It's all the fault of Adam'?"

The *otun* asked the *osi*, and the *osi* asked the *balogun*, but none of the king's officers could answer the questions.

"Go, then," said the king to the *otun*, "and bring the woodcutter to me. If he has been unjustly treated, I must know about it."

As soon as Iyapò entered, he prostrated himself, laying first his right cheek and then his left cheek on the floor of the piazza where the king sat.

"Well," said the king, "I am curious. What is your name?"

"Sire," replied the woodcutter, shaking with dread, "my name is Iyapò."

"Iyapò . . ." the king murmured into the *Irù kèrè.* "Your name means 'many troubles.' But why must you blame *Adam* for your misfortunes?"

"S-sire," stammered Iyapò, "I have heard of Adam, who long ago disobeyed God and ate a certain fruit in the Garden of Eden. If Adam had not disobeyed, we would all be happy in the Garden. And I would not have to work so hard now to earn my daily food."

"Hmmn," said the king, looking long at the thin, ragged woodcutter. "You work hard, and you have but little. Surely it is unfair that someone else's disobedience should cause you so much grief. Something must be done for you.

"*Otun,*" the king continued, "have Iyapò washed and dressed in clean, new clothes. Find a room somewhere in my palace where he can live. And take away his ragged clothes and his bundle of wood. From now on, he will lead a new and happy life."

Then, turning to the woodcutter, the king nodded. "From this day forward," he said, "you may call yourself my brother. Everything that I have you may share. You can do anything you want, except"—and he looked directly into Iyapò's eyes—"*except* open the green door near the end of the hall. That door you must never open."

"Oh, sire," answered Iyapò joyfully, "why should I want to open the green door? You have already given me everything I could want or need. I have food and clothing and shelter. Surely I should be contented!"

For many weeks the woodcutter enjoyed his good fortune. He ate three meals a day, instead

of one. Indeed, he ate so well that he became
fat. He wore the fine new clothes the king had
given him. When he tired of these, the king's
servants provided him with robes even more
handsomely embroidered.

Day after day, week after week, he amused
himself in the king's palace, until he had quite
forgotten how it felt to arise early in the morning
to cut wood. He no longer remembered the
pain of hunger, or the sting of disappointment.
He had almost forgotten that he had ever been
anything else but the king's brother.

One day as he strolled through the palace,
he chanced to notice the green door. "Ah," he
murmured, "that is the door I must not open.
How curious! I wonder what lies behind it?"
But he knew he must not open it, so he turned
his back upon it.

Day by day, however, he stopped often and
oftener before the green door. Without his
seeming to choose that hallway himself, his feet
led him there, and he wondered more and
more about what lay behind the door. Each time
he came closer to putting his hand upon the
latch, but still he hesitated.

Then one day the king was called to another part of the town on business. "Iyapò, my brother," he said, "look after the palace in my absence. I may not be back until well past dinnertime."

"Look after the palace," Iyapò murmured as the king left the compound. "If I am to look after the palace, surely I am responsible for the room behind the green door. After all, I am the king's brother. Why should *any* room be forbidden to me?" Looking carefully here and there to be sure he was not watched, Iyapò went quietly to the green door. He listened, with his ear pressed against the door. There was not a sound from the other side. "I'll open it just a little bit," he decided, "and then I'll close it tightly again. The king will never know. But I *must* discover what is inside."

Lifting the latch, he peered into the room. He blinked, and looked again. There was nothing at all in the room except his own ragged clothes and his bundle of wood! As he stood there, disbelieving, a small gray mouse hiding in a shadow in the far corner suddenly ran between Iyapò's feet and out into the hallway. "Ah!" exclaimed Iyapò. "It must be the *mouse* that the king is so careful about! I must catch him and put him back, or the king will know that I have opened the green door." Hastily latching the door, he set out after the mouse.

Up one hallway and down another raced Iyapò, with the mouse in sight but just beyond his reach. Soon he began to huff and puff. All those weeks of good eating had made him too fat to run easily. And he stumbled again and again on the wide skirt of the handsome robe he was wearing. Pausing a moment, he took off the robe and flung it on a bench. Then he ran

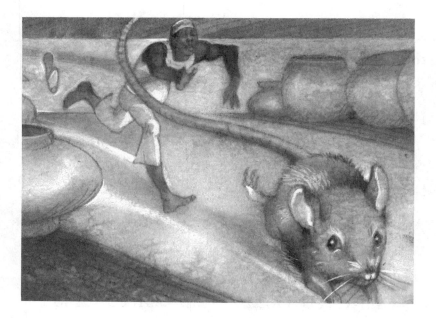

again, faster, losing his right shoe here, his left
shoe there. *Still* he could not catch the little
gray mouse.

"What are you doing?" The voice of the king
rang through the hall.

Iyapò stopped running. His heart pounded till
it seemed as if the very walls must hear it.
The king! But he was not to return until well
past dinnertime. . . . Suddenly Iyapò knew fear.
He fell to his knees before the king.

"Oh, sire," he began, "I am sorry about your
mouse."

"My *mouse?*" the king asked, puzzled. "I have
no mouse. And what are you doing, running

through the palace without your robe, without your shoes? The brother of the king must walk proudly, with dignity."

"You—you see, my brother," Iyapò stammered, "the mouse ran out when I opened the green door, and I knew that—"

"The green door!" exclaimed the king. "So you opened the green door. Was that not the *one thing* I told you that you must not do?"

"Oh, yes, sire, it *was*," Iyapò agreed. "And I wasn't going to open it. But day after day it was there, and day after day I wondered about it. And as the king's brother—"

"As the king's brother," the king interrupted, his eyes blazing with anger, "you felt you must be the king himself. And you thought *Adam* was disobedient! What *he* did should have taught you caution."

Iyapò prostrated himself before the king, right cheek on the floor, left cheek on the floor. Then, "What is your will, O king?" he whispered.

"Go to the green door," said the king, his voice low now, and sorrowful. "Take your ragged clothes and your bundle of wood. It is not other people's good wishes which can make you happy, but your own destiny. Sell your wood,

since work is the cure for poverty. But know
this, my friend: your misfortune is not the
fault of Adam."

Iyapò arose. He walked on his bare feet past
the fine shoes he had lost, past the handsome
robe he had flung aside, to the green door.
Opening it, he put on his ragged clothes, which
scarcely covered his stout figure. Lifting the
bundle of wood to his shoulders, he walked out
of the cool palace into the dust and heat of the
market. "Wood! Wood for sale!" he called.
"Wood! Good wood for sale!" But no matter
how many times he cried his "Wood for sale!"
there was no longer a mention of Adam.

"That's just how I felt when I first came to this field."

TWO WISE CHILDREN

Robert Graves

A boy called Bill Brain, a minister's son, lived in New England near the sea. One Tuesday morning in summer he went for a walk through the fields, picking blueberries into a tin can. Half a mile from home he passed a big house which some newcomers to the town had just bought. They were Colonel and Mrs. Deeds and he had first met them on the Sunday before, outside his father's church. Colonel Deeds watched birds, and Mrs. Deeds drove fast cars. Avis, their only daughter, had fair pigtails, a sunburned face, white teeth, and a snub nose. Bill felt shy with girls, having no sisters. But something about Avis

had struck him at once. It seemed as though he
had known her for years and years, and as though
they shared a big secret. And he guessed that
she felt the same about him because her smile
wasn't just a polite smile of welcome, but one that
meant, "Oh, there you are at last!" Avis was
eight, and Bill two years older!

The day before, when Bill had awakened from
a bad dream, he remembered that Avis had come
into it, and that he had dreamed the same thing
two or three times since Christmas. He couldn't say
exactly what had happened in the dream, except
that he was being watched by a huge, jeering
crowd while some big black animal tried to kill
him, and that suddenly Avis flew down from a tree
and said, "It's all right, Bill. The bandages are in
father's medicine chest." He thought to himself,
"What a crazy dream!" Yet it still seemed real
to him in a way and he couldn't laugh it off. He
couldn't even bring himself to tell his mother
and father about it at breakfast.

Well, now it was Tuesday morning. And as
he passed the Deeds's big house with the blueberry
can slung around his neck, he suddenly said
to himself, "How could I have dreamed about Avis

long before I met her? Or did I just dream that I had already dreamed the same thing two or three times before?" Bill could see nobody in the Deeds's garden, and he didn't like to shout "Avis, are you there?" So he went on towards Robson's farm, which lay hidden behind a wood. The best blueberry bushes grew on a small rocky hill nearby and he went up it, picking fast into the can, which was already half full. A few minutes later he reached the top and saw something very curious on the other side.

There stood Avis
on the back of Robson's white horse,
with one foot lifted like a dancer's, her arms
spread out, and a hay rake balanced upright on
her chin, while the horse galloped around
the field!

"That girl must have worked in a circus," he
thought. But in case she might not like being
watched, he went back behind the hilltop, picked
blueberries for another five minutes or so, and
then came up again whistling loudly. Avis had got
down from the white horse and now sat on a
rock with her head bent over some work or other.

•••

She heard Bill's whistle.

"There you are at last," she said.
"I expected you five minutes ago.
Where have you been?"

But Bill was looking at a small
square of white linen which
she held crumpled in her hand.
"Is that what you have been sewing?"
he asked. "Let me look!"

"Oh, it's not worth anything," Avis said.
"This is the first time I've done needlework.
I borrowed mother's colored silks. It's taken me
most of the morning."

"What else have you done?"

"Oh, eaten a few blueberries and tried riding
Farmer Robson's horse."

"I suppose that was the first time you ever rode
a horse?" Bill asked, to tease her.

But Avis said seriously, "Yes, the first time ever,
but I got along quite well."

Bill took the crumpled square of linen from
her hand, and found on it the most wonderful
needlework he had ever seen. It was a silk picture
of flowers and butterflies sewn in about thirty
different colors with hundreds of tiny stitches.

···

Only one flower and half a butterfly were not yet finished.

"Did you copy a pattern?" Bill asked.

"No," said Avis.

Bill looked her straight in the eyes. He said, "I saw you riding the horse. I hope you don't mind. And now there's this marvelous needlework. Explain, please. . . ."

"Oh, I didn't mind being watched by *you*," said Avis. "And there's nothing much to explain, really. I wanted to do a circus act, so I just did it, because I knew how. And I wanted to make this needlework picture in colored silks, so I just did it because I knew how."

"Oh, I *see!*" said Bill.

"What do you see?" asked Avis.

"I see what's happened to you. It's like what happened to me last spring in a field near our house. I was alone, and the dogwoods had just begun to flower, and hundreds of birds sang, and the world seemed changed and *right*."

"Yes," said Avis. "That's just how I felt when I first came to this field. Go on!"

Bill went on, "Suddenly I found that I knew everything. I had only to tilt my head a little and ask myself any question I pleased, and the answer came at once."

"What *sort* of things?"

"Well, I had often wondered who first built our house and when he built it. So I tilted my head and knew that a Scotch blacksmith called Sawney Todd and his son Robb had built it in 1656. And somehow I knew that if I dug down four or five inches under my left heel, I'd find an old gold brooch belonging to Ruth Todd, Sawney's wife. So I cut out a piece of turf with my knife and found the brooch. It had 'R.T. 1654' scratched on the back."

···

"Did that scare you? *I* got a scare at first by things going marvelously right like that. I'm used to them now."

"It did scare me a little. Then I went home and there was my Uncle Tim arguing with Father about some law business. They had a lot of papers spread on the table, written in very difficult English. Uncle Tim was being rather rude to my father, so I said, 'You're wrong, I'm afraid, Uncle Tim.' And I picked the papers up, read out one of the most difficult ones to him, and showed him just where he had made his mistake. They both looked at me in such surprise that I got all red and explained, 'You see, I know everything today.' Father frowned at me for boasting, but Uncle Tim laughed and asked, 'All right, Bill, if you know everything, what horse will win the big race on Saturday?' I tilted my head, and then told him, 'A big black horse called Gladiator will win. It's ridden by Sam Smile.'"

Avis interrupted. "I don't *know* everything, Bill; it's just that I can *do* everything. It's a bit different. Do you still know everything?"

Bill sighed. "No, I don't, Avis. That's what I want to warn you about, if you don't mind.

Take care not to let anyone but me into your
new secret. I made a terrible mistake over mine."

"What sort of a mistake?" Avis asked.

"It had to do with money. My Uncle Tim went
off to town and bet a hundred dollars that
Gladiator would win the race, and it did. He made
a thousand dollars from the bet, and gave me
a ten-dollar bill for myself, and told all his friends
about my knowing everything. One of them
asked me what horse would win the
next big race. I tried to tell him,
but somehow no answer
came. Then I hoped that I'd
know if I saw a list of all
the horses that were
going to run.

The man showed me a list, but still I couldn't tell
him the winner, so I guessed a horse called
Clever Bill—and it came in last! That was in May,
and I have never since felt that I know
everything. I'm sure I lost my magic
by taking the ten dollars.
Magic and money don't mix."

Avis said, "You mean,
Bill, that I oughtn't
to tell anyone,
even my mother,
that I can do
whatever I like?
Just in case her
friends try to make
money out of me?"

Bill nodded. "I'm sure
that's how it is."

Avis looked a little sad as
she said, "Thank you, Bill. I'll have
to change my plans. I'd thought of winning
the hundred-dollar skating competition at the
New Year Ice Carnival—I haven't ever skated,
but it looks fun. And I'd thought of teaching my
dog to sing real songs while I played the guitar.

•••

And I'd thought of growing a new red flower
with my name written in white on its petals,
which would come out only on June tenth—
that's my birthday."

"Mine too," said Bill.

"And flying round and round the White
House at Washington, just to amuse the
President. Like this . . ."

Avis suddenly jumped
into the air, glided around
a big maple tree,

picking a leaf from the top branch as she went by, and then lay down in the air about three feet from the ground as if she were on a sofa. She said, "I'm not showing off, Bill, I promise. I'm just telling you how easy it is for me to do things."

"*Please* be careful, Avis," said Bill. "If your magic went away, you'd feel so lost and empty inside."

"But it's far more fun to do things like this if someone is watching and knows that I really can do them. I'm lucky to have *you,* Bill. I trust you."

"Oh, I wish, I wish, I wish I hadn't taken Uncle Tim's money," said Bill. "I wish I knew everything again. It would make life so much easier, especially school."

"Maybe you'll get the magic back one day," said Avis.

"I doubt it," said Bill. "Anyhow don't lose yours! Don't let your father and mother find out that you aren't just an ordinary little girl. Don't fly up to your bedroom through the window when they may be looking. Use the stairs! And I'd better keep this bit of needlework hidden. Your mother might ask questions about it."

Avis gave Bill a hug and said, "I *do* like you, Bill. You're my favorite friend of all. Thank you, thank you!"

Bill said, "By the way, Avis, did you dream of me before we met?"

"Oh, yes, ever since I can remember. I guess that's because we have the same birthday."

She ran off, and Bill thought, "I'm glad she didn't fly home. Farmer Robson's in the next field and might have seen her."

Avis kept Bill's advice all that summer. They saw a lot of each other. Since she didn't really care about making money, or showing off to strangers, she might never have lost her magic but for another stupid mistake of Bill's.

•••

It happened like this. One day he thought, "Maybe I could learn Avis's sort of *doing* magic, although I've lost my own *knowing* magic." He walked towards Robson's farm, and there he saw Robson's bull: a big, mean, black brute which was kept in a special field with stone walls and a padlocked iron gate. Bill had read about bullfights. He knew that in Spain the bullfighter goes into a ring where thousands of people sit watching all around. When the bull rushes up, the bullfighter holds out a red cape and steps aside to let the bull charge it instead of him. Then he keeps on making the bull charge his cape, time after time, all around the ring, and everyone cheers. And then . . .

"I'll try it,"
Bill said.
He climbed
the gate, walked
towards the bull,
and took off his brown
jacket to act as a cape—but
forgot that he was wearing a red shirt
underneath! Bulls hate that color, and instead of
charging the jacket which Bill held out, Robson's
bull went straight for the shirt, knocked him
down, stuck a horn into his leg, and tossed him
high in the air.

That would have been the end of Bill, if his dream hadn't come true. Avis suddenly appeared when he had been horned three times. Somehow she tamed the bull, laid Bill (who had fainted) across the bull's shoulders, jumped up behind, and made the bull gallop back to her home!

When they got there, she called to Colonel Deeds for help. But he was bird-watching somewhere, and Mrs. Deeds had gone shopping in the station wagon. So Avis grabbed bandages and all sorts of first-aid stuff from the family medicine chest. Then she bandaged Bill's wounds, stopped the bleeding, and put Bill into the back of her mother's sports car.

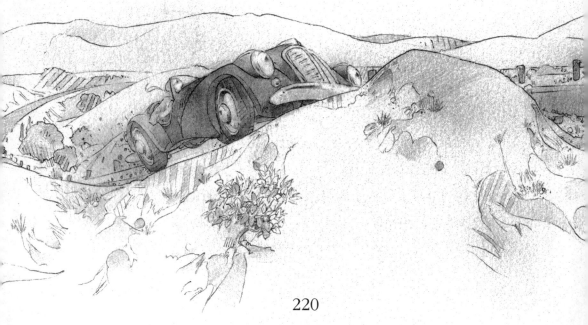

In spite of the state police who tried to stop her at the crossroads, she drove ten miles at full speed to the nearest hospital, where the doctors took charge of Bill. She had forgotten about the bull, which ate most of the roses in the garden and made holes in the lawn with its hooves.

Avis had no chance of keeping the news quiet. The police wanted to know how she had managed to drive her mother's car so fast and well, and the doctors wanted to know who had bandaged Bill's leg in such a clever way, and Farmer Robson wanted to know how his bull had gotten over a locked gate! Reporters came from all the

newspapers and asked her more questions and more questions, and she kept on saying "I don't know . . . I don't know," because she had promised Bill to be careful, and it was true that she didn't know *how* she had done it all without learning. They took photographs of her and put her name in the papers as EIGHT-YEAR-OLD GIRL WONDER.

Soon the Governor called at the Deeds's house and asked to see Avis. Mrs. Deeds was very proud of the visit and let the Governor pester Avis with more questions until she got tired of answering "I don't know, I don't know." At last she burst into tears and said, "Oh, *please* go away, or you'll spoil everything! Can't you leave me and my magic alone?"

"Oh, so you do it by magic?" said the Governor, giving her a huge box of candy. "How very interesting! You mustn't cry! Will you come and show us some magic at my little girl's birthday party next Saturday?"

And before Avis could say "No, I won't! It's a secret," Mrs. Deeds answered for her. "Of course, Mr. Governor, my daughter will be *delighted*." This was how Avis lost her magic.

ACKNOWLEDGMENTS

All possible care has been taken to trace ownership and secure permission for each selection in this series. The Great Books Foundation wishes to thank the following authors, publishers, and representatives for permission to reprint copyrighted material:

The Little Daughter of the Snow, from OLD PETER'S RUSSIAN TALES, by Arthur Ransome. Published by Penguin Books Limited.

The Ugly Duckling, from IT'S PERFECTLY TRUE AND OTHER STORIES, by Hans Christian Andersen. Copyright 1938 by Paul Leyssac; renewed 1966 by Mary Rehan. Reprinted by permission of Harcourt Brace Jovanovich, Inc.

Ooka and the Honest Thief, from OOKA THE WISE: TALES OF OLD JAPAN, by I. G. Edmonds. Copyright 1961 by I. G. Edmonds. Reprinted by permission of Macmillan Publishing Company.

The Brave Little Tailor, from GRIMMS' TALES FOR YOUNG AND OLD, by Jacob and Wilhelm Grimm. Translation copyright 1977 by Ralph Manheim. Reprinted by permission of Doubleday, a division of Bantam, Doubleday, Dell Publishing Group, Inc.

Jean Labadie's Big Black Dog, from THE TALKING CAT AND OTHER STORIES OF FRENCH CANADA, by Natalie Savage Carlson. Copyright 1952 by Natalie Savage Carlson. Reprinted by permission of HarperCollins Publishers.

Caporushes, from ENGLISH FAIRY TALES, by Flora Annie Steel. Copyright 1918 by Macmillan Publishing Company; renewed 1946 by Mabel H. Webster. Reprinted by permission of Macmillan Publishing Company.

It's All the Fault of Adam, from THE DANCING PALM TREE AND OTHER NIGERIAN FOLKTALES, by Barbara Walker. Copyright 1968 by Barbara Walker. Reprinted by permission of Four Winds Press, an imprint of Macmillan Publishing Company.

ILLUSTRATION CREDITS

Brock Cole prepared the illustrations for *The Brave Little Tailor.*

Diane Cole prepared the illustrations for *Jean Labadie's Big Black Dog.*

George Cruikshank's illustrations for *The Master Cat* are from GEORGE CRUIKSHANK'S FAIRY LIBRARY, first published in 1870 by Routledge, Warne, and Routledge. Reproduced courtesy of the Newberry Library.

Leo and Diane Dillon prepared the illustrations for *The Little Humpbacked Horse* and *Ooka and the Honest Thief.*

Tom Feelings prepared the illustrations for *It's All the Fault of Adam.*

Wanda Gág's illustrations for *The Fisherman and His Wife* are from TALES FROM GRIMM, by Jacob and Wilhelm Grimm, freely translated and illustrated by Wanda Gág. Copyright 1936 by Wanda Gág; renewed 1964 by Robert Janssen. Reprinted by permission of Coward, McCann & Geoghegan. Reproduced courtesy of the Regenstein Library at the University of Chicago.

David Johnson prepared the illustrations for *The Little Daughter of the Snow* and *Two Wise Children.*

Mary Jones prepared the illustrations for *The Monster Who Grew Small.*

Emily Arnold McCully prepared the illustrations for *The Ugly Duckling.*

Ed Young prepared the illustrations for *Caporushes.*

Cover art by Ed Young. Copyright 1992 by Ed Young.

Text and cover design by William Seabright, William Seabright & Associates.

When Bill got out of the hospital, none the worse, she blamed him for having spoiled her fun. But she *had* saved his life, which was the important thing; and he would always be her favorite friend.

Besides, in some ways it was a relief to be ordinary again, like Bill.